Murder in the Cotswolds

Murder in the Cotswolds

A. B. GUTHRIE, JR.

HOUGHTON MIFFLIN COMPANY · BOSTON

1989

For information about permission to reproduce selections
from this book, write to Permissions, Houghton Mifflin
Company, 2 Park Street, Boston, Massachusetts 02108.

Library of Congress Cataloging-in-Publication Data
Guthrie, A. B. (Alfred Bertram), date
Murder in the Cotswolds / by A.B. Guthrie, Jr.
p.   cm.
ISBN 0-395-41456-3
I. Title.
PS3513.U855M8   1989   88-39434
813'.52—dc19   CIP

Printed in the United States of America

P 10 9 8 7 6 5 4 3 2 1

For Ruth K. Hapgood,
that helpful editor

AUTHOR'S NOTE

There is no Upper Beechwood in the Cotswolds, and no Lower Beechwood, either, but there are dozens of villages like those imagined ones I've written about. A beautiful country, the Cotswolds. I hope I've made that plain.

I am forever indebted to Carol, my wife, not just for her patience, though Lord knows I'm grateful for that, but for her assistance and encouragement.

Murder in the Cotswolds

Chapter One

"YOU CAN TELL they're Americans, Geeta," Charleston said.

"It would be pretty safe to bet on it, the number who visit Great Britain."

They were seated at the Carver's Table in Edinburgh's George Hotel. The room was big, rather elaborate, somewhat imposing, and not very busy right now. He said, "Interesting, different people's eating habits." A vacant table stood between them and the five diners he was talking about.

"Quit ogling them, Chick."

Beyond them at the head of the room were glass-shielded counters with assorted vegetables and haunches of meat on them. Two carvers stood with knives in their hands.

Charleston's eyes weren't on them.

"One of those women is not bad looking, the small one."

"Chick!"

There were just two women in the group, the nice-looking one and a bigger, square one. A little man with wire-rimmed glasses was talking with gestures, busy as an auctioneer. One of his listeners nodded occasionally. He might have been the teacher and example at a fitness school. The other was bigger, coarser, with a thick chest and heavy arms.

"Please, Chick, quit staring," Geeta said. "You're not Sheriff Charleston in Midbury, Montana. You're on vacation. Remember?"

He turned to her, smiling. "It's the detective in me. But sure I remember. These days will be with me as long as I live."

He thought of them, then quoted, " 'And always have goodness and joy waited on my comings and goings.' "

"I can quote things, too, like, 'Oh, we shall have a golden day to spend, to follow shining ways that have no end.' "

"Yes, Geeta. Yes," he said, putting his fork down. All their free and easy days, days of looking, seeing, learning something of another people, driving slow while sight and sound entered them, and all the days golden and all the ways shining.

He put out a hand and she gave hers to him, and he said "Geeta" into her eyes.

The waiter had brought coffee. Chick freed his hand slowly and sipped. Her father had called her Geet, short for Marguerite. Charleston had added the "a," thinking to soften it. He said, "I love your new tweeds and you in them."

She fingered her new jacket. "I like them, too, I don't have to say." She took a bite of the cake she had ordered, and for a moment they were silent. Then, after another swallow of coffee, he said, "So it's on to the Cotswolds, on to the home of your ancestors, on to the family tree."

"Don't exaggerate, Chick. I'd like to know more about my lineage, but I'm not set on tracing myself back to the primal gene. It's more I want to see Upper Beechwood and how and where my grandfather lived. In what circumstances. What surroundings. He always said it was a heaven of a place. I wonder if the house is still there?"

She laid the fork on her plate, touched her mouth with a napkin and went on, "We have another day here. We've seen a lot of Scotland but haven't yet climbed to the castle right here in the city."

"I catch the drift. I get the angle. All right, I'll limp along. I'll pant up the inclines and puff up the stairs, and we'll see how royalty lived if it kills me."

"You poor old man."

"That's me, girl. Got a song ready to sing me goodbye, or you could sing about Glencoe again?"

The gloomy Glencoe country popped into his memory, and the lines she had sung in her soft and rather husky voice.

> "Cruel was the foe
> That raked Glencoe
> And murdered the house o' MacDonald."

The coach driver had recited something about Glencoe but in accents so burred, so foreign, that Charleston had whispered to Geeta, "That's English? The Lord will have to have an interpreter for the man's prayers."

Now, the meal finished, he said, "Early yet. Let's go sit in the lobby and watch the human procession."

"You mean watch the folks traipse by."

"Yeah. There's something in the air fancies up my language."

"Right now I have to find the powder room, as we call it. They're not so fancy hereabouts. They call it a toilet, which is just what it is."

The party of five had risen from the table. He and Geeta followed them, and while he signed for the dinner, Geeta left, saying, "See you in the lobby."

Geeta found the little woman just ahead of her. They entered the compartments and came out almost together and walked to the water basins and the mirrors above them. While she touched up her face, the woman said, almost as if to herself, "It's such a chore. Blusher, lipstick, eye pencil, hairdo." She turned, her mouth half-smiling. "Doesn't it get to you sometimes?"

"Sometimes."

"Why do we do it? Out of vanity? To look attractive for other women? For men who may not even notice? Why?"

Geeta arranged a lock of her hair. "Mostly for ourselves, I suppose. Goodness, my hair's a mess. But don't you think it's nice to look nice?"

"I can't imagine your looking any other way. American, aren't you?"

They were done with their make-up and moved away from the mirrors.

"Yes," Geeta answered. "Both of us. Aren't you all?"

"All of us but one. Mr. Smith is still British though he's lived in the United States for years."

"This is our first time in Great Britain. We're from the west."

"Where?"

"Montana."

"For goodness sake! That's where I was born. In Glendive."

"Well!"

"I remember hardly anything about Montana. My father failed there as a sheep rancher and then made out well as a businessman in the east. I was just a little girl."

Geeta said, "It's been nice talking to you, but I must go. My husband will be waiting. Tomorrow we climb to the castle. Then it's on to the Cotswolds. You've heard of that part of England?"

"For heaven's sake! Heard of it? We're going there, too, to a little place called Upper Beechwood."

Geeta's mouth had fallen open, she realized when she closed it. "Now you'll be telling me you have reservations at the Ram's Head Inn?"

"Where else in that little place?"

Geeta shook her head. "Who would believe it?"

"Who would? It's like something ordained, isn't it? We'll see you there then. My name's Drusilla Witt."

"Mine's Marguerite Charleston."

They strolled out to the lobby and stood looking around until Geeta said, "Here comes my husband now. Sorry to keep you waiting, Chick."

"Not too long."

"I want you to meet Mrs. Witt, Drusilla Witt. Mrs. Witt, my husband, Charles Charleston. She's from Montana, Chick."

"So long ago I can hardly remember."

"And that's not all I have to tell you, Chick."

"Let's find some chairs. Won't you visit a while, Mrs. Witt?"

"I see my people over there." She laughed a little. "I guess they won't miss me."

Charleston led the way to chairs arranged around a low table. When they were seated, Geeta told him about the coincidences, ending with, "That takes some believing, doesn't it? All of it, I mean."

"Not all of it's so strange. Some, but not all."

"Oh, Chick! What isn't coincidence?"

"For thirty years and more Montana has had a population of about three quarters of a million, sometimes slightly more, sometimes slightly less. That means a lot of birthings, a passel of kids, we might say."

Geeta egged him on with, "So far, so good, Professor."

"Well, now, with so many babies born, wouldn't you think the population would grow? It hasn't, though. It's remained pretty stable. That means people leave Montana, go to live in New York, California, Chicago, or settle abroad. So what's so extraordinary about two Montanans meeting somewhere else? Stands almost to reason."

"One man down, two to go," Geeta interjected.

"I'll grant it's quite a coincidence about going to the Cotswolds, and to Upper Beechwood at that. But it's natural that both parties register at the Ram's Head. No place else to stay. That's according to the guidebook."

It was rather quiet here in the lobby — just the drone of conversation of people seated away from them, just the movements of the bellmen and clerks at the desk whiling away time until the next flurry.

"You make things sound pretty simple," Mrs. Witt told him. "May I ask what you do when you're not on vacation?"

"I'm a public officer."

Geeta broke in. "Don't be so mysterious." She turned to Mrs. Witt. "He's the sheriff of our county in Montana."

A coach must have stopped in front of the hotel, for people began flooding in — men and wives, women with children, men with briefcases, and bellmen with baggage, all intent on their private business, all looking somewhat absent-minded with purpose.

He heard Mrs. Witt saying, "A sheriff. That sounds exciting. Indians and cowboys and chases on horseback."

"Oh, sure, and a man for breakfast every morning."

"Now, Chick," Geeta said.

"I know when I'm being had," Mrs. Witt answered. Her laugh was light, a laugh with no amusement in it, Charleston thought.

"So may I ask about you?" he said. "Is it business or pleasure?"

"It's business, at least partly. I don't know how much. I hope not for long. You see, my husband has a twin brother, a chemist who owns a small shop in Upper Beechwood. My husband wants him to sell out and throw in with him." She added, with what Charleston thought was wistfulness, "That much I do know."

"They were born in England then?" Geeta asked.

"No. In the United States. Walter and William. But William married a visiting English girl and then, perhaps because she wished it, moved to England. He's been a British subject for a long time."

She sat for a moment, touched her head with one hand, and went on, "Who knows whether he'll move or how long it will take to persuade him? You know how identical twins are.

Closer in a sense than man and wife." She swallowed the little
catch in her voice. "Yes. Closer. They visit back and forth, no
often, and keep up a steady correspondence. But I'm jus
chattering away."

She laughed lightly again, a surface laugh. Her whole
manner was light, yet somehow not light. Something, Charles
ton reflected, was eating on her. Some disappointment. Some
misted dream. Or was she just shallow? Or was his mind
making things up?

As if she had forgotten, Mrs. Witt went on, "Mr. Smith
now, he's here at least partly on business. Something to do
with an estate."

"A sort of group holiday for you then?"

"More or less. Mr. Post — that's Mr. and Mrs. Post over
there — has been in business ventures with my husband, and
so has Mr. Smith sometimes. I'm sure I'm mixing you up, but
Mrs. Post — Eleanor's her name — and Mr. Smith are sister
and brother, and both were born in the Cotswolds."

She took a handkerchief from her jacket pocket and
twisted it in her hands. "My husband's into so many things,
here and there, off and on. He's so old-fashioned. Business
for men, home and church and coffee parties for the ladies.
He never mentions business matters to me."

Which was probably why she talked as much as she did,
Charleston reflected, why she had stayed talking to them so
long. Charleston found it easy to think so. She was, he
decided, something more than pretty. She had that look of
sad and even innocent loveliness that got to a man.

She rose from her chair. "You'll have to excuse me. They'll
be wondering."

She walked, a small, straight figure, to a husband who
wouldn't tell her anything.

Charleston took Geeta by the hand and brought her up.
"Bedtime, or just about. There's a wanting woman, Geeta."

"Wanting?"

"More than she has. More maybe than she's ever had. Some kind of denied comfort. Some failed dream. She needs consoling."

"You old romantic. Haven't you heard of come-ons?" She lifted her face, a hint of amusement in it.

"Just a sucker, huh?" he replied. "But keep in mind that you may be wrong."

"Yes, Chick," she said, still smiling. "But don't you go getting ideas."

He answered her smile and squeezed her arm. "I already have an idea, but it's not about her."

Chapter Two

"THESE ENGLISHMEN DRIVE as if the devil were eating their tailpipes," Charleston said.

"You're doing all right," Geeta answered, and after awhile said, "Wasn't Burford a disappointment, even if it did introduce us to the Cotswolds?"

"And Bibury?"

"All golden stone and slate roofs and a river running by. I loved it."

A pheasant winged up before the car and flew into the woods, and Charleston said, "Ring-neck," before his mind returned to their subject. "People in these villages sure don't seem to get around much. That waitress at Burford rarely went to Oxford, she said, and it's only twenty-some miles away. No wonder, maybe. Nice enough where they are."

"At least in Bibury. Why leave Eden? Did you know Eden was so green? Look at those hills and pastures."

"Just sit tight, and tourists will come and leave their money."

"This is no day to be cynical."

It sure enough wasn't. The April sun was kind, the sky

clear, and the air good to smell. And he thought of Stonehenge, and a sort of gentled time was in him. For the moment he was glad he wasn't on a case back in Midbury. Tea and scones and clotted cream, against the greasy food of cattle-town cafes.

They came to a hill, and Charleston slowed the car, looking for a lay-by. At the top he pulled into one and switched off the engine.

Below them lay a valley, a vale as they termed it, and beyond it the hills and the hollows flowed away and away, a study in misty greens with sheep feeding in a small clearing. "There," Charleston said. No need to point.

"A dream world," Geeta said, "and it stretches so far that the eye can't go to the end."

It was no time to say the entire Cotswolds were not as big as their county back home, no time to say the atmosphere did the trick.

"It's so peaceful."

No time, either, to remind her there was hardly an inch of it that hadn't been soaked in human blood. All the blood-letting seemed to have reached resolution now, in this still serenity, in a yellow stone on a green field with a ewe and a lamb resting by it.

"Sing, Geeta. A song would go good."

"Even if your grammar's bad?"

"Don't I have a right to be wrong?"

"Sure, silly. All right. I don't know why. It's not appropriate, but a song has been running in my head. It's known as 'The Cradle Song.'

> "I'm here by the fire
> Without heart's desire
> And rockin' the cradle
> That nobody owns.
>
> "I'm sittin' and sobbin'

And rockin' the cradle,
And rockin' the cradle
That's none of my own.

"Hi ho, hi ho, hi diddlely ho-o.
Perhaps your own daddy
Will never be known.

"I don't remember all of it."

"Good enough. Good enough."

"Sometimes it's called Joseph's song."

"Reminds me of 'The Streets of Laredo.' "

"Joseph of the Bible, dummy. And get your succession right. 'The Cradle Song' came first."

"Yes, ma'am."

He started the car and let it laze along. "There's a village, I swear, every jackrabbit hop. Each one, I reckon, a sort of enclave."

"But all so easy to look at. So in keeping with the land. With that stone they look as if they lived in the last rays of the sun."

At a small town called Chipping Campden they parked the car and strolled to a pub, where they ordered what the natives called a plowman's — crusty rolls, cheese, chutney, and pickled onions.

They returned to the street and entered a little antique shop. "You have some nice old china," Geeta said to the woman inside, "but no flow-blue. Don't you ever stock it?"

The woman smiled, "When I have the chance, and that's not often. American dealers pick it up so fast, and at such prices!"

Geeta purchased a couple of small figurines.

Outside, they paused to look at the market hall with its arches and gables. "Built in 1627," Charleston said quietly, feeling again the long years of time.

"Not old by English thinking," Geeta reminded him.

"No. Just American. We're such a young country."

It was going on to seven o'clock when they reached the Ram's Head in Upper Beechwood. Charleston turned off the motor, and they sat looking for a moment. "Nice enough place," he said. "From the outside, anyhow."

"It's pretty. Yellow stone and slate roof and all. And it's big enough without being too big."

"Twenty rooms, maybe, and some cottages in back. Let's go in and see."

A small woman stood behind the registration desk.

"We have a reservation," Charleston told her. "We're the Charlestons."

"Oh, yes," she said, smiling. "Welcome, Mr. and Mrs. Charleston. We've been expecting you. I'm Helen Vaughn."

"Owner and proprietor, it says in the guidebook." Charleston returned her smile.

"Also maid of all work, it seems sometimes. How long will you be staying?" She had put the registration book in front of Charleston.

"About a week," he answered. "Allow a day or two either way. Long enough to learn something of the Cotswolds."

"I hope you'll be pleased. Our season is just about to open. Our special chef who comes in the summer will arrive soon. You'll like his dishes. Dinner tonight in about half an hour." She rang for a bellman.

Turning away from the desk, Charleston saw that the small lobby was empty save for a man who sat holding a cane. The man nodded and smiled.

The bellman, a scrawny youngster, arrived and wheeled out a truck, and Charleston led him to the car and helped him load. "Car be all right here?" he asked.

"For now 'twill be. Until the season opens."

Geeta was investigating their quarters when Charleston and the bellman arrived with the bags. "It's nice," she said. "Plenty good enough."

The bellman left with thanks and his tip.

"Cream and brown," she went on. "I like these quiet, faded colors, so different from what we see at home."

"Did that woman, Mrs. Vaughn, seem a little flustered to you?"

"You notice things like that. I seldom do. Now we'd best hurry, Chick, or we'll be late for dinner."

They were about to sit down at the table to which a young and rather pretty waitress had directed them when she appeared again, now with the Edinburgh party of five.

"Why," Mrs. Witt said, coming forward, "hello, again. I was about to think you had changed your minds about coming here. This is our third night."

"We loafed through the Lake District," Charleston explained.

"And made several side trips," Geeta added.

"But here," Mrs. Witt said, beckoning, and went on to introduce her companions — Mr. and Mrs. Post, Oliver Smith, and last of all, her husband.

Mr. Witt asked, his eyes friendly behind the rims of his glasses, "Are you going to stay a while?"

"About a week, we think," Charleston answered. "What about you?"

"A few days. We're not quite sure yet."

Geeta said, "You must be finding plenty to do then?"

Mrs. Witt answered, "Oh, my, yes. Seeing the sights of the Cotswolds. Shopping. Antique hunting."

"Mostly antiquing," Mr. Witt said with a smile.

"Don't you go on about that," Mrs. Witt said pleasantly. "How about that fishing you and Ben have been doing?"

Mr. Post put in, "On the worst stretch of water ever rented."

"We'll do better the next time," Mr. Witt assured him.

"I doubt we'll have time for a next time," Mr. Post said. "I hope not."

"Take it easy, Ben," Mr. Witt told him. "It's not every day I get to visit my brother."

Mr. Post turned away, his back half to them, as if tired of the company. Mrs. Post hadn't said a word. She stood silent, grimly imposing. She might, Charleston thought, have been the heroic representation of stoic womanhood after a hard day.

Nor had Mr. Smith spoken, beyond a syllable of greeting. Geeta asked him, "Don't you like to fish, Mr. Smith?"

"No."

Mr. Post took time from his contemplation of the far wall to say unpleasantly, "The lone wolf likes lone-wolfing."

At last Mrs. Post spoke. She put a hand on her husband's arm and said, "Now, Ben."

The group separated then and took different tables. Seated, Geeta said, half-whispering, "That man, Smith, he undressed me."

"Hardly."

"His eyes did."

"No harm done." He smiled. "Can't say I blame him."

Several other people were entering the room, welcomed by another waitress. The first waitress came back to the Charleston table, saying, "Good evening, my name is Rose. May I take your order?"

They settled on sole, and until their orders came looked around the room. It was beamed and attractive, in what Geeta observed was a restrained way and to her liking. A bus boy was clearing a table left by earlier diners. He was husky enough to wrestle a steer. A boyish smile brightened his face when the first waitress passed him.

With a glance at the nearby table where Mr. Witt seemed to be holding forth, Geeta said, her tone low, "I'm glad we're not members of a party, Chick. I may go shopping or have tea or something with Mrs. Witt — your Mrs. Witt — but it's better, just the two of us."

"My Mrs. Witt or not, it wasn't in my mind to join forces. We might get tied up."

Chapter Three

"SEEN ENOUGH of the Cotswolds?" Charleston asked. It was afternoon. He had turned the car more or less in the direction of Upper Beechwood and was just poking along.

"In only two days?" Geeta answered. "It's not seeing now so much as just feeling, so I haven't had enough yet." She sighed. "But I suppose we must get back to Upper Beechwood. It's so expensive, paying for rooms at two places. We should have checked out for a day or two at the Ram's Head."

"Now, Geeta, I keep telling you, nobody takes a vacation to save money. The idea is to blow what you've saved. So what's in your mind, ma'am?"

"Oh, nothing, Chick."

"Out with it."

"I liked Bourton-on-the-Water so much."

"The Old Manse?"

"And the river running by. What's it called?"

"The River Windrush. We'd just say the Windrush River, but the British got a way of their own. Anyhow, you want to spend another night there?"

"Could we, Chick?"

"Of course. No need to ask me. What am I? Big Honcho?"

He turned the car to the right at a roundabout, not caring where the road led. It was enough just to be rolling along in the sunshine. By and by he'd find the way back to Bourton-on-the-Water.

"I don't suppose our friends will leave in our absence," he said just to have something to say.

"Friends? The assorted five? I would call them acquaintances."

"Amendment accepted."

"That chesty number. That Oliver Smith. Don't call him friend. I told you. He tried to eat me with his eyes."

"Your fault. You look good enough to eat."

She gave his leg a pinch. "Don't dodge. I tell you he's up to no good. I don't like him. I keep wanting to deflate him, say with a hat pin."

"You're such a savage."

"It wouldn't hurt me to say goodbye to the rest, including your Mrs. Witt."

"That's a sly poke. I never staked a claim there."

"I'm teasing you."

"I know, but you worked up quite a head of steam just the same."

"That was when I was talking about the man Smith."

He pulled over to the side of the narrow road to let a car pass. Then he reached over and took her hand. She turned to him, smiling. "I like you to be attractive, Chick. So there. You can't help it, anyhow. But I admit I can get a little jealous. By the way, I'm beginning to like you in that hat."

"Cap, not hat. Better than those wide-brimmed things we wear in Montana. Better in the winds."

"Cowboy hats do give you shade, though."

"If you can keep them on your head. And you can curl the brim up and use it as a cup, that is if you happen to find water. And you can fasten it on your head with a drawstring under your chin, and the first blow will cut your throat."

"End of discourse?"

"I won't bore you by finishing."

So, he reflected as they eased along, they talked of this and that, talked of nothing much or fell silent, not feeling the need to talk, and that was as it should be. A lazy, satisfying serenity.

"Tomorrow or next day," she said, "I'll get around to tracing my ancestry, but it's nice just to get the feel of the country, to enjoy, for his sake in a way, what my grandfather enjoyed. It's all soft yellow right now, not just the buildings, but the gorse, the forsythia, and the daffodils. And even the stone fences look as if they grew here."

Better to look at than barbed wire, he admitted to himself. Gentler. In keeping with the gentle country. Admitting as much, he felt again the bite of Montana suns and the push of Montana winds, felt them again and missed them.

She went on, "I can feel things, too. The press of old times, I guess I could say the weighted years, but the feeling isn't unpleasant, just sort of sad, like an old memory."

"I know," he replied, "but now it appears we're entering Stow-on-the-Wold. Strange name, but seems like a nice little place."

"Stop the car, Chick. Park it, please." She was pointing out the window. "See that store? I have an idea."

He found a parking place on a side street. As they reached the main street, Geeta exclaimed, "I love the way the fruits and vegetables are put on display outside. And they look clean, ready to eat."

They dodged an old woman with a cane, and another with three little tagalongs, dressed as if for church. They made Charleston remark, "The English sure take care of their kids."

"Not so loud, Chick."

"They don't like compliments, huh?"

"Never mind. Here we are."

It was, sure enough, an attractive store. Geeta led the way to the men's section. "Now we're going to shop for you."

"I have enough."

"If you think I'm going home with all the goodies, think again. How many kilt skirts have I bought? How many jackets? How many sweaters?" A clerk had come up smiling. "No, sir, mister. It's your turn."

She spoke to the clerk, a young man with amusement in his eyes. "It's for my husband," she said. "I think we know what we want."

Charleston shrugged. "She means she knows what she thinks I want."

"Be still now."

The clerk said, "I'll be happy to show you."

"Fine. Moleskins? Do you have the shirts and coats?"

"Now why do I want moleskins?" Charleston asked.

"Warmth." Then, to the clerk, "Can you fit my husband?"

"Yes, I'm sure."

"And what colors do they come in?"

"Only green, madame."

Charleston groaned. "Green. Lead me to Robin Hood."

"Now, Chick, not that kind of green. You'll look fine. And think about Montana winters. Think about being warm."

"Sure. Green and cozy."

But when he was outfitted, Charleston lagged to a mirror. They didn't look too bad, those duds, and they were certainly warm. He said, "Thank you, Geeta."

She wore a pleased look, one that meant, didn't I tell you?

"Now," he said, back in the car, "I'd better try to find my way back to Bourton-on-the-Water."

Chapter Four

DETECTIVE CHIEF INSPECTOR Fred Perkins of the Gloucestershire C.I.D. felt grumpy. It was just his luck to get this assignment, a case of murder in a moldering little place called Upper Beechwood on the outskirts of the county. Add to the bloody luck the fact that the victim was an American.

It was early morning on his day off, but here he was, ready to go. No sense in stalling, no matter the outlook. Not quite ready, though. He had to clean up after his lonely breakfast. He got up and went to work on the dishes, recalling that Martha did things like that when she was alive. Ten years ago, that was.

A good woman, Martha, he thought as he washed and dried, a good woman and an indifferent wife. Secure in her church and her God, she was as passionless as a potato. Neither had she wanted to know about his work. It was as if knowledge of his involvement with sinners would soil her soul. A good thing they couldn't have children. Papa to some pious little bastard of her rearing!

He put the last dish away. Even the long years since her death hadn't cured him of the sore of disappointment in her, hadn't freed him of the old exasperation at her indifference. Refused as often as he had been, a man festered. What he needed was a woman, he reflected, thinking of the one who came to his flat on occasion.

He hung up the tea towel and waited. His bag was packed, his briefcase at hand. Sergeant Goodman would pick him up any minute now. A fine young officer, Goodman, though not so young in the service, come to think of it. Almost a son in a sense. He'd have him to help this time. He hitched in his chair, hating the prospect before him. An American with a knife in him. An American among a group of five. More public interest because he was an American. Headlines. And Superintendent Hawley, that meddling bastard, would be sure to stick his nose in.

Well, who cared? Who the hell cared? Do your work. Keep your temper if you could. Suffer the goddamn years to pass and retire with a pension. Great prospect.

That would be Goodman at the door now. Perkins called, "All right," opened the door, and started to pick up his luggage. Goodman beat him to the bag, saying, "I have it," and they walked together to the car.

Once beyond the town, Sergeant Goodman said, "Nice day. I like it out in the country."

Perkins answered, "It would be nicer but for this bloody case."

"You'll solve it, sir."

"Perhaps. Superintendent Hawley and us."

Goodman turned a grin on him. "Don't worry, sir. I think we can handle his highness."

"He's sure to put his oar in. Might be there already."

"No, sir. He was still at headquarters when I left."

"Learn anything more about the case there?"

"I didn't learn anything about it."

"That rustic constable gave a sketchy report. An American stabbed in his bed last night. Name of Oliver Smith. He and four other Americans had been at the Ram's Head Inn for a week. The maid found him in bed, a knife in his back. No money in his wallet. No other signs of disturbance. There you are. Make the most of it."

"Yes, sir." Goodman whistled a snatch of "Amazing Grace." When his eye wasn't on the road, it was on the fields around them. That was a thing about Goodman. No time for low spirits with so much of interest around him. A damn good man, Goodman, even if his cheerfulness seemed out of place, out of keeping with his own feelings.

Upper Beechwood was more of a village than he remembered — a couple of pubs at least, two shops in sight, a chemist's, and ahead of them the Ram's Head. Townspeople stared from entryways as they approached. Not to be wondered at. It wasn't every day the place had a murder.

Goodman pulled up in front of the inn. At least the place looked neat and inviting. A thin young man grabbed at his sleeve, saying, "Aren't you Detective Chief Inspector Perkins?"

"They call me that."

"I'm a reporter. What can you tell me about this case. Murder, isn't it?"

Perkins jerked his sleeve free. "Not one bloody thing."

He ignored the gazes of half a dozen people in the lobby and went straight to the desk. A small, trim woman, who gave her name as Vaughn, Helen Vaughn, greeted him. She was dressed in brown and had brown hair, a suitable color, it flashed in his mind, for a case that promised no brightness.

"Detective Chief Inspector Fred Perkins," he told her and produced his credentials, then introduced Sergeant Goodman.

"Yes, Inspector," she replied as if at the tail end of breath. "It's so humiliating, a violent death in my hotel."

She ran out of steam at the finish, and the lines of pain appeared on her face. She put a hand up to her chest and with the other steadied herself against the counter.

Perkins said sharply, "Are you all right? All right, ma'am?"

She took the hand from the counter, opened a drawer,

took a pill from a box, and put it on her tongue, her movements unsteady. "Just give me a minute," she said, and after a pause went on, "This terrible thing. It upsets me so. My heart acts up."

"Shouldn't you lie down?"

"No. No. I'll be fine now."

"Have other officers been here?"

"You're the first." She added, "Are others coming?" as if she hoped not.

"I'm afraid so." He paused, "Constable Doggett is expecting us."

"I expect he's in a cottage outside. I set it apart for your investigation." Because, he thought, it was better than having officers under foot in the lobby or a mobile crime unit parked next to the inn. "I'll show you the way."

"You stay. That's one thing we should be able to find."

"Go out this door and turn left. It's the first cottage on the right."

Followed by Goodman, he strode to the door, taking little note of the watching eyes and the questioning silence. Outside, the reporter grabbed at him again. "Inspector, please. I've talked to Constable Doggett."

Perkins walked on, saying over his shoulder, "Then you know more than I do." He paused after another step. The poor sod was just trying to do his job, as he was himself. "When I learn more, you'll be informed."

"Thank you, sir. Remember my name. Charlie Evans."

A uniformed man stood in the cottage doorway, his face wide in a smile. "I'm Constable Doggett, sir."

"Detective Chief Inspector Perkins." He gave one shake to the man's eager hand. "And Detective Sergeant John Goodman."

"I've tried to fix things up," Doggett said, showing them in. There were four chairs in the room, one of them a high-backed rocker, and a sofa, a desk with two telephones and a sheaf of blank paper on it, and a file drawer.

"Fine," Perkins said. "I'll want to hear more from you later. Now we'll have a look at the body."

"It's at the undertaker's, sir."

"At the undertaker's!"

"Yes, sir."

"Not here at the hotel, in the room where it was found?"

Doggett gulped, started to speak, and brought up his hands as if to explain.

"Good God, man, you let the body be moved?"

"I — I — didn't see any choice, sir."

"No choice? You ignored a prime rule of investigation. What kind of an officer are you?"

Doggett looked down at his moving hands, his face torn with distress.

Before he could answer, Perkins added, "Let the body lie until after a proper examination. That's the right procedure."

"I'm not a detective constable, sir. Just a constable."

Perkins wouldn't let his tone soften. "All right. Why no choice?"

"Rose Whaley, her that found the body, and Mrs. Vaughn, you must have met her — well, they was in a state, Mrs. Vaughn in particular. When she learnt of the death, her face went white. She fell to the floor. I thought she was going to die. She has a tricky heart to begin with."

"So?"

"I tried to get the doctor, but he was out. I laid her out and put a cold pad on her head, and she come to, sort of, and what she said is still in my head. Her voice was like a scream. 'Get it out, George! Out now! I'll die!' Then she said, kind of under her breath, 'A dead man, killed, in my hotel.' "

Doggett looked up, his eyes pleading, "That's it, sir. I thought I was going to have two bodies on my hands. Two, one dead because I hadn't took charge."

"No use to cry now. It's too late."

"I guess I been in over my head."

"I guess you have. What about the man's clothes?"

"I got what he didn't have on."

"And sealed the room?"

"With everything out of it, I didn't see a reason to do that. Mrs. Vaughn even had the bed stripped."

"Sergeant Goodman," Perkins said, "please go seal the room. Then we'll have a look at the body." And then, he told himself, there'd be time to question those bloody Americans.

and turned around. The man before him wore a blue suit and a tie of lighter blue. There was something military in his appearance. He motioned Charleston to one side. "May I have a word with you?"

"Sure. My wife, too?"

"Perhaps later. Now if you'll just come with me."

"See you soon, Geeta."

The man led the way outside, around a corner, saying as they walked, "I'm Inspector Perkins of the Gloucestershire C.I.D."

"What's the trouble?"

"Just come along, please." He opened the door to a cottage in which three men sat. He said, "Mr. Charleston, here are Detective Superintendent Hawley, Detective Sergeant Goodman, and Constable Doggett." He had inclined his head to indicate the men he introduced. "Please be seated, Mr. Charleston."

The superintendent sat behind a desk. He had shallow gray eyes and a face like a wedge, in which the mouth made a crosswise nick. Charleston glanced at the sergeant, who had taken a seat in the rear, a note pad before him. He was large and appeared capable. The constable looked like nothing much.

Charleston took the seat indicated, opposite the superintendent. Perkins sat at his side.

Hawley looked at the notes on his desk and inquired, "You are Charles Charleston." He raised his eyes. A smirk touched his lips. "Can that be correct?"

"It's correct."

There was no depth in those gray eyes, no human kindness in the pinched mouth. If there was a soul anywhere, it was in hiding.

"You are an American?"

"Yep."

"Just touring Great Britain?"

"Yep."

Chapter Five

IT WAS WELL INTO the afternoon when Charleston slowed for the turn into the Ram's Head. It had been a calm and peaceful day, and in his head were the memories of small villages, golden in the sun, of shaded lanes and the good smells of green and flowering things. But, nearing the inn, he said, "Some kind of trouble here, Geeta."

"Oh?"

"Two cars, official, looks like, and there's a dead wagon."

"Dead wagon?"

"Meat wagon. Carriage for corpses."

"That's dreadful talk. Somebody's died?"

"I guess. I'll park over at the side."

Inside, Mrs. Vaughn was registering a couple with two fretful children. The man turned, the pen in his hand, and demanded, "Can't you hush those kids?" The woman tried to. Americans probably, from their accents. Both worn out with kids and travel.

Facing Charleston, Mrs. Vaughn put a shaking finger to her lips, cautioning him to be quiet, he supposed, not knowing about what. It was then that he felt a tap on his shoulder

Hawley's gaze went to Perkins. He gave a playful nod as he said, "We have a one-syllable man here."

Perkins said shortly, "He's answering."

"Four syllables," Charleston said. "What's the trouble?"

"First things first," Hawley said, turning. He tapped on the desk with the end of a pencil. "Where were you last night and early this morning?"

"I spent the night with my wife at Bourton-on-the-Water. At the Old Manse. I suggest you check there. We took our time getting back here today."

"But you were registered here at the inn?"

"You know how us fool Americans are. Rich. We just throw our money around."

Hawley tapped harder on the desk. "This is serious business, Charleston. A man has been murdered."

"Oh. Why didn't you tell me?"

"I've told you now. What do you do? What's your line of work?"

"I'm a public officer."

"That's hardly specific. What kind of officer?"

"Sheriff of my county."

Hawley rolled his eyes, maybe to indicate thought. "Sheriff? That's almost an obsolete term in England. What's your function? Collecting taxes? Serving papers?"

Charleston glanced around, at Perkins, who gave him a little nod, at Goodman, who had raised his pencil, and at Doggett, who must have adenoids. Then he answered, "Same function as yours. Law and order."

"Any murder cases in your experience?"

"A few."

"Naturally, you solved them all."

"Naturally. With good questions and maybe a little brain work."

Hawley put the pencil away with a certain air of decision. "I'll tell you, then, that an American has been murdered.

That makes the case unusual. It arouses the authorities. It puts us in a spot. The American Embassy will be on our necks. A right mess."

"Here at the inn." It wasn't a question, but Hawley answered. "Yes. In his room. Knife in the back." Hawley bent forward. "His name was Oliver C. Smith. Do you know an American named Oliver C. Smith?"

"No."

"What? Never even shaken hands with him, a lodger here like you and a compatriot?"

"Not even once. But I did meet an Englishman by that name."

Hawley's mouth fell open, what little there was of it. "Now say that again. An Englishman?"

"You heard me."

"But how would you know?"

"Hearsay. In your shoes I'd look at his passport."

Hawley drew in a whistling breath. It came out saying, "Jesus humble Christ! His passport!" He glared at the other men. "Doesn't anyone around here ever have any bloody ideas?"

Perkins spoke then, his tone acid. "No one but Mr. Charleston."

"Where is the bloody thing? Doggett, where?"

"Yes, sir. It's locked in the hotel safe along with his wallet and stuff."

"Get it!"

Doggett knocked over a chair getting out. There was a silence until Hawley said, "Doesn't that bloody constable know an English passport when he sees one?"

"Probably not," Perkins answered. "Probably he didn't even inspect it."

"An Englishman," Hawley said almost to himself. "Hmm."

The door burst open with Doggett saying, "Here it is, just like I said." He gave it to Hawley.

Hawley hardly needed to examine it. He nodded his head, then nodded again. "English all right. No Yankee embassy on our necks." A little smile touched his mouth. A real smile, Charleston thought, would have cracked a lip.

"Only a poor damn Englishman," Perkins said, his tone still acid. "No big trouble. Still, it's a case, wouldn't you say, sir?"

"Of course. It remains to put the suspects through the strainer." Hawley didn't know sarcasm when he heard it. Either that, or he didn't heed it.

"Now I'm beginning to wonder if the others are Americans." Perkins said, as if the question had just struck him.

"Make sure of that," Hawley told him.

"Oh, do you really think I should?" Perkins answered. It seemed to Charleston that he came as close to sneering as he dared.

"You'll find they're American citizens," Charleston cut in. "I know that much."

"Those damn Yankees," Perkins said. "Begging your pardon, Mr. Charleston. I might as well have kept mum for all I could get out of them. Oh, I have their signed statements, but, hell — " He made an impatient gesture with one hand.

"I thought they spoke English," Superintendent Hawley said and waited on Perkins's reply.

"It's English, all right. But Jesus. They're a strange breed. I suppose you don't find it so, Mr. Charleston?"

"Nope. Not with most."

Abruptly Perkins turned to Hawley. "A bloody good idea. Listen to this. I want Charleston on my side. He can talk to those Americans. An ex officio helper, that's what I mean."

Hawley shook his head, not vigorously. "Our department doesn't need outside help."

"We need all the help we can get."

Hawley considered and then answered almost in a sneer, "Yeah. Maybe you do. Maybe you can use him. I wouldn't, but it's your case."

Charleston put in, "I won't be here very long. A week's stretching it."

Ridges had shown at the point of Perkins's jaw, but now he said in cold even tones, "Not 'use' him. Wrong word. Benefit from his help." Now he turned to Charleston. "I'm sorry. It seems I'm taking a lot for granted."

"I said I was here only briefly."

A look came on Hawley's face, a look of thought or calculation, maybe of cunning. Who could read the mind of a hatchet? "I suppose it wouldn't hurt," he said softly.

"I won't have much time," Charleston reminded them.

"Two can take the blame easier than one," Hawley said. His eyes were mean.

Perkins was quick to ask, "How's that?"

"I mean in the event the case isn't solved."

"I resent that." A red flush climbed into Perkins's face. "Since when have I dodged my mistakes? Since when have I put the blame on others? I take my knocks when they come."

"There's been quite a lot of that lately," the superintendent said wryly.

Perkins said, "That's shit."

"All right, Inspector. All right. Let it go," Hawley said. He rose abruptly. "Have it your own way. Keep in mind it's your case, like some others I might mention." He stepped toward the door. "I'll be off. The boys will be through, and we'll get the body to Gloucester. You'll get the reports when we have them." He halted at the door. "Don't let murder interfere with your dinner."

With the door closed, Goodman exploded. "That bloody bastard. Goddamnit, sir, a little more of that, and I'll take him on."

Perkins put out his hand, his anger fading. "I know, my friend. I know. But let's cool down." His attention went to Charleston. "I hope, sir, you'll lend us your help. I'd be grateful."

Charleston hesitated for only an instant. Then he said, "Long as I'm here."

Chapter Six

CHARLESTON WENT to his room, where he found Geeta reading the guidebook. She tossed it aside and said, "It's about time."

"Patience, Geeta." He moved over and kissed her.

"You've been up to something," she said, as if she knew it.

"Not up. Hooked. Beached."

She waited, her eyes on him.

"Murder," he told her. "Murder here at the inn."

"Who was it?"

"Our friend Mr. Smith. Found in his room early this morning with a knife in his back."

"That's just horrible, Chick." She paused and went on, "And what was the bait they used to get your help?"

"I wouldn't call it bait. A law officer's got to assist if he can."

She sighed. "Even if not on his own turf?"

"I doubt murder knows any boundaries."

"Clues?"

"None. The four Americans are the prime suspects."

"Not the Witts!"

"Who knows? Come along. Let's eat. We're late."

There were few people at dinner, and those few were well along with it. The four from Edinburgh were not among them. Observing the proprieties probably, Charleston thought.

The waitress, Rose, who had served them before, came for their orders. She appeared subdued, with no greetings or smiles for them. Indeed the whole room was quiet, murmurous only, as if in the presence of death. The new chef was the exception. As the door to the kitchen swung open, Charleston caught a glimpse of him. In his white apron and tall chef's hat, he seemed perky and satisfied. He was chunky, reminding Charleston of what a deputy had once proclaimed: If you want good food, find a fat cook.

With Rose hardly out of earshot, Geeta said, "Tell me more, all you know."

He went over the afternoon, giving the facts and his impressions. Before he had finished, the girl came with their dinners. "Sketchy," he said at the end. "I'll know more presently. I promised to see Perkins again tonight."

"But, Chick, without knowing all about the case, how can you question the Americans?"

"I thought of that. It's sort of in for a penny, in for a pound."

"You'll be totally involved."

"I hope I can play hooky once in a while."

She said, "So it's goodbye to our vacation."

"Now, Geeta. Geeta. Is that fair?"

It was an instant before she answered. "No, Chick, it isn't." She put out a hand to touch his. "I'm sorry. I've had almost three weeks of doing just what I wanted."

"What *we* wanted."

"I was being plain selfish."

"Just human, Geeta. Just human."

He went on, "I could hardly refuse Perkins when he asked. And the superintendent was such a jackass. Hold up. Wrong word. Denotes stupidity. The English would call him a bloody bounder. And besides, you'll be busy chasing your ancestors."

She laughed then. "I knew I had lost you when I heard the word 'murder' in the lobby. But it's all right. You're you, and I'm glad of it."

Charleston nodded, feeling a great tenderness in him. "You're the best, Geeta, the very best in the world."

When they had done with their coffee, he told her, "I really must go now. I don't want to keep Perkins waiting. I'll have more to tell you later."

Perkins, waiting in a cloud of pipe smoke, rose from his chair in the cottage and offered his hand. "Goodman and I just got here. Ate at one of the pubs. Leave it to Goodman to spot the good places."

Goodman, seated a short distance back, signaled acknowledgment of the remark.

"Sit down, Mr. Charleston. Sit down." Perkins motioned with his pipe and reseated himself behind the desk where Hawley had sat earlier. He pulled on his pipe and puffed out a stream.

"I didn't know you smoked," Charleston said pleasantly.

"Not in the presence of the most high," Perkins said, grinning. "He has an allergy. Says he has, and makes a fuss."

"Some people do."

"Not you?"

Charleston took a thin cigar from his pocket, saying, "This answer you?" He lit up.

"Better air, tobacco smoke and all, with old poison-breath absent."

"Not for good, though?"

"He'll be sticking his beak in, never fear, but the fact that the victim is not an American has dulled his appetite. No big doings."

"He eats headlines," Goodman interjected. "Got a real addiction."

"You're pretty sharp with him sometimes," Charleston told Perkins.

"Not to worry. He's impervious to gibes."

"Take a kick in the arse to impress him," Goodman volunteered.

"Let's leave this dirty subject," Perkins said, "and get on with the case. Some of the facts you already know or have suspected from what has been said."

Charleston nodded.

"All right, then. Just to review things." Perkins interrupted himself to relight his pipe. "Oliver C. Smith, an Englishman and guest here at the inn, was found dead in his bed at about ten-thirty this morning. A girl named Rose Whaley, who waits table and helps when she can with the rooms, discovered him. She ran, screaming I suppose, to the registration desk. Mrs. Vaughn, proprietor of the inn, called the constable, George Doggett, and Doggett called us."

Perkins put his pipe aside but only, Charleston supposed, for the moment. "There's an immediate difficulty. There's no scene of the crime."

"But . . ."

"I know. A crime was committed, so there has to be a scene. But Doggett, that greenhorn, allowed the body to be removed to the mortuary, and Mrs. Vaughn, upset no end by the fact that a murdered body had lain in her inn, had the room dusted, wiped down and vacuumed immediately and then had the bedclothes thrown in the washer." Perkins put a hand on his pipe, "All that was done before our arrival."

Charleston found his own smoke had gone out. He re-lighted the cigar and waited.

"To go back a bit. The body was only partly dressed. His trousers and jacket were on a chair. Nothing at all in the pockets, but a wallet lay on the floor. It contained nothing but a driver's license and some credit cards. No bills. No silver. No money at all."

"Suggesting robbery?"

"You think so?"

"Sure. A possibility, that's all." Charleston studied the smoke he blew out. "How long had the man been dead?"

"Our information — it's an estimate — is not before midnight last night and not after two o'clock this morning. Mr. Smith was with a party of Americans. You know that. You know them, Mr. and Mrs. Walter Witt and Mr. and Mrs. Ben D. Post. They're suspects, of course, as who isn't, but I got nothing useful out of them. Perhaps you can."

"That's just perhaps. I've hardly more than met them. From the little I've seen, I'd say Post is a difficult customer. Probably Smith's sister, Mrs. Post, too. The Witts seem more open."

"Post was the most contrary. You can see their statements if you want to. Those of Mrs. Vaughn and the girl who found him are there, too."

"I doubt I ever saw Smith open his mouth. My wife didn't like him. He stared at her, not innocently, it seems. Did you know that Smith and Post both once wore beards?"

"You knew them from before, or saw them?"

"I saw them first in Edinburgh some days ago, and the skin tones showed where the beards had been."

"You think that significant?"

"It could mean they are on the dodge."

Perkins said, "That might not matter to our case."

"It may not. But I could call Washington and maybe pick up something? I'm thinking, you know, about that saying, when thieves fall out . . ."

"Good idea. About Washington. Should have thought about it myself, but it's not exactly our problem. I'll get headquarters on it."

Perkins rose and paced the room, and Goodman said, "Too early for sweat now, Inspector."

Perkins returned to his chair and plumped his butt in it as if that act of decision might settle other matters.

Charleston asked, "What staff members live in the inn?"

"Only three. Mrs. Vaughn, Rose, and a night man who answers the bell if it rings. He has a cubbyhole just beyond the registration desk. Hold on, though. The chef, name of Armand, arrived just day before yesterday. He has his own room. That's all, except a family friend who helps out at the inn when needed, but she lives at one of the cottages. She leases it."

"No signs of a break-in?"

"Not a one. The door to the murder room was unlocked." At Charleston's hesitation, Perkins said, "Don't be shy about questions. I might forget something."

"But I seem to be giving you the business."

"So what? Ask away, my friend."

"The entrances to the inn, are they locked at night?"

"We're told the front door is locked at midnight, but there's a bell for late-comers that the night man anwers. The side and back doors are supposed to be locked at night, but we haven't inquired enough about them."

"Another question. What about guests last night?"

"Six men, besides the Smith party. Sales representatives and businessmen, apparently. I have their names and addresses."

"Locals?"

Perkins shook his head. "Locals wouldn't be likely to stay here."

"Dumb question."

Perkins smiled briefly. "They were from Birmingham, Manchester, London, and Bath. Headquarters will check on them if, in his wisdom, Superintendent Hawley considers it important. We want to see the man from Bath, a chap named Peter Tarvin. He got quarrelsome in the bar last night, and Doggett put him in jail. He needed help in subduing him. And guess who helped? One Oliver Smith."

"Is Tarvin still in jail?"

"No, confound it! Doggett let him out this morning, since, as Doggett put it, he had kind of sobered up. That was before

Smith's body was found. Not to worry, however. We've located him. He'll be on hand in the morning."

"Anything on the other lodgers?"

"Not a thing. They left early. They can wait. There are hotter prospects right here."

"An in-house job, you think?"

Perkins nodded. "From present indications." He put his pipe aside. "The preliminary questions didn't get us anywhere much. The Americans all are as innocent as spring lambs, to hear them tell it. Likewise with the girl, Rose, and the others we've had time for. But bear in mind that the questions were more or less superficial. Since you'll be questioning the Americans next time, I imagine you'll want — well, to bear down, so to speak."

"Whatever the occasion calls for."

"There's one other thing. Goodman will be staying at the inn, and you can get in touch with me through him."

Goodman looked up, grinning, catching Perkins's attention.

There was a certain sheepishness in Perkins's manner. "It's this way. Doggett came to me. Seems he inherited a big house and got it divided into two sections, both complete, soundproofing between so his phone won't disturb tenants. But no luck with tenants so far, so he invited me in. The damn man was so eager, so anxious to put himself in a good light that I felt sorry for him and said yes."

Goodman chuckled. "Sympathy will do you in if you're not careful, Inspector."

Perkins said, somewhat meekly, "They're very nice quarters."

Sympathetic in turn, if not with Doggett, Charleston said, "An advantage. You'll be right there if Doggett gets alerted."

"Yes. That's enough for tonight, I suppose," Perkins said, sighing. "I'm afraid it's too late for a beer."

"No sir," Goodman spoke up. "I put some in the cooler just in case."

"John, I forgive you your impertinences."

Perkins and Goodman drank silently, their faces thoughtful. At last Perkins shook himself and said, "It's early days yet. Up and at 'em tomorrow."

Charleston said nothing until his beer was finished. Then he stood and said, "Goodnight, men," and heard their replies as he went out the door.

Geeta was asleep. He listened to her deep and quiet breathing and in the dim glow of a night light saw a tendril of hair curled on her forehead. To touch it back would be to awaken her.

He shed his coat and walked quietly to the small dressing room for his pajamas. But before he could take them from the shelf, he heard a light knocking at the door. He tiptoed there, opened it, and laid a finger across his lips at the sight of his visitor.

Goodman said, almost in a whisper, "I'm sorry, sir, but could I talk to you for a minute?"

Charleston nodded, took his coat from the chair, and let himself out, careful about closing the door. "Where?" he asked.

"Somewhere private, sir. Not the cottage. He might spot us."

"My car then? It's around at the side."

Goodman nodded and led the way out.

In the car he said, "The inspector wouldn't thank me for this. He's too proud."

"That doesn't tell me much."

Goodman shifted uneasily and waited for words to come. "I'm maybe a bloody fool," he said, "but maybe not. Maybe not."

Charleston waited for more.

"All right," Goodman said after a long pause, "you know the inspector and you know the super, but you don't know it all."

"Hardly."

"The fact is that the super is out to get the inspector, on any grounds he can trump up. The inspector deserves a lot better than that. He's a good officer."

"I feel sure of that."

"And Hawley, begging your pardon, sir, is a right bastard, as mean a man as you are likely to meet."

"So?"

"There's nothing fair about it. Inspector Perkins should be the superintendent and Hawley the inspector, or lower down. It turned out the opposite. Inspector Perkins was slated for the promotion, but Hawley got it."

"How?"

"By sucking up to the chief constable. Also, he's Hawley's uncle."

"Nepotism."

"Favoritism, anyhow. The chief constable, now — "

"Wait a minute. How much brass in your outfit?"

"Brass?"

"Officers then. Inspector, superintendent, and then what?"

"There's the chief superintendent and the chief constable."

"Lots of generals in your army."

"Seems like to you, I suppose. What I was saying, the chief constable was fine and all right once, but he's got old, older than his years, and he doesn't listen to anybody much except that nephew of his."

"Who has nothing good to say about Perkins?"

"That's it. And look here, why do you reckon Hawley agreed to let you in on the case? I'll tell you. So if we break it, you'll get the credit, and if we don't, Inspector Perkins will get the blame."

"Neat arrangement," Charleston said dryly.

"Some of the juices went out of Inspector Perkins when he didn't get that promotion," Goodman said, partly to himself. "He used to find some joy, some spirit in his work, and now he just goes along, all business, without a laugh in him. They gave him a tough job in Cheltenham, and Hawley pulled him off of it before you could say scat. No explanation, but the word went around that he wasn't getting anywhere with his investigation. But Inspector Perkins didn't kick or mention facts. Not his way. He keeps it all inside him, boiling, and one day the boiler will explode. Pressure cooker, like. I worry about him. A man can stand so much, then he blows up."

"That would suit Superintendent Hawley?"

"Too right it would. Look at the situation here. Hawley lets Perkins have one man. Me. We should have at least two detective constables, asking questions, doing some house-to-house, finding if any strangers, suspicious characters, were noticed by the locals. But what does the inspector have instead? Me, and that poor muttonhead, Doggett, who has other chores to do, like any police constable."

"So Hawley wants him to fail."

"Sure. Wants reason to pull him off, get him discharged or demoted to a lousy desk job. And Inspector Perkins puts up with it, has to, I reckon, while the pressure in him mounts. No safety valve, either, none unless we solve this case quick. He won't kowtow to Hawley."

"Would you have him do that?"

"No. No. But I can hope to help keep the lid on."

"All right, Sergeant. And thanks. But why are you telling me all this?"

"Mr. Charleston, it's because maybe you can help. I don't mean just by questioning the Americans. I mean all the way."

"Don't worry about that. When I agreed to do the questioning, I did it knowing I'd have to be completely involved."

"It's not that Inspector Perkins isn't a capable detective. He's damn good. You have to believe that. But I'm remembering what my father used to tell me: two heads are better than one."

"Let's count yourself and make it three."

Goodman gave a fleeting smile, put his hand on the door handle, said a thank you and, as he left the car, threw back, "We have to solve this case. We just have to."

Chapter Seven

GEETA SHARED AN EARLY BREAKFAST with Charleston, early though a good many customers were already in the dining room. "Today," she said, "I start on my family line —that is, if they've left any traces." For the day she had put on a gray woolen skirt and a cherry-colored cardigan.

"Good hunting," Charleston said, pushing back from the table. "Time for me to go."

"Chick, you be careful now."

"Sure. Coming?"

She only hoped he wouldn't be getting himself into any danger.

She stopped in the lobby to talk to Mrs. Vaughn, smiling in return to Charleston's goodbye salute. Mrs. Vaughn stood behind the desk, looking frail but somehow resolute. "Good morning, Mrs. Charleston. Something?"

"I'm looking for word of my ancestors. I mean I'm tracing my family, or trying to. Maybe you can help. My maiden name was Hawthorne. Do you know of any Hawthornes around here or who once were around?"

"No. I'm sorry. But we don't go back very far ourselves. Just twelve years."

"Who might know? Some old man or woman, if you can think of one?"

Mrs. Vaughn tapped a pencil against her front teeth as if as an aid to thought. "There's the old grocer. Ebersole is his name. He's very old, though quite alert, but he's not a native so probably can't help you. Then there's old Mrs. Williams, but the poor thing is not right in the head these days. There's Mr. Ross, but he's bedridden and doesn't see company. Oh, yes, here's a possibility. Mr. Steele. Mr. George Steele. He must be pushing ninety, but his head's clear, so I'm told. He has a housekeeper, Mrs. Brownlow. Why don't I call and see if I can arrange a visit?"

"Would you, please?"

Mrs. Vaughn turned to the telephone. The call completed, she said to Geeta, "Mr. Steele is an early riser. He's installed for the morning and will be pleased to see you."

"Fine, and thank you. Now where does he live?"

"At the very end of the street. Last house on the right. That way." Mrs. Vaughn pointed the direction. "Nothing's very far in our village."

"I wonder if it's going to rain?"

"It might. The sky's a trifle gray."

Geeta turned. "I'll get my umbrella." It was a new one, small, bought in Edinburgh. With it in hand, furled, she set out. You didn't see umbrellas in Montana often, she thought. Too much wind, too little rain. In London during a shower a whole busy street had suddenly blossomed with them. Even under gray skies the Cotswolds buildings looked warm and inviting.

A small, tidy woman opened the door of what must be the Steele home. "Do come in," she said. "We were expecting you. Mrs. Charleston, isn't it? My name is Mrs. Brownlow." She led Geeta into a small parlor, where an old man sat with a robe around his knees. The room with its worn furniture looked cozy. A well-trodden oriental rug lay on the floor.

The old man raised a thin arm and said, "Howjudo, Miss. Have a chair there."

"I'm doing fine, thanks," she said and sat down. "I hope you are."

"Well as can be expected, as the hospitals say when they're expecting the worst. I'm ancient, that's all."

"You know my name?"

"Charlton, wasn't it?"

"Charleston. Marguerite Charleston."

"American, by the sound of you."

"Yes."

"Putting up at the Ram's Head, huh? Mrs. Brownlow tells me murder's been done there. Another American."

"No. An Englishman traveling with Americans."

"Americans are a murderin' lot." His old eyes questioned her, perhaps asking for denial. A shrunken arm came from underneath the blanket. In the thin skin of his temple, she could see the pulse in a blood vessel. She imagined he had been a robust man until age withered him.

"We have our full share of killings," she answered. "But the most famous murder cases happened in England."

He smiled. It was a friendly smile that revealed false teeth. "I like answers like that," he said. "Now just what's on your mind?"

"My maiden name was Hawthorne. It's the Hawthornes I'm interested in. They lived here in Upper Beechwood. It's a Cotswold name, I was told."

Mr. Steele extended a hand. The fingers were bent and knobby. "You're wrong there, ma'am. The Hawthornes came from Scotland, somewhere near Fort William. Went back there, too, after the boys left for America."

So that was the end of her search, Geeta thought, not letting herself sigh. No going back to Scotland now to make up what she had missed. She said, "You knew the family then?"

"The boys and I played together. The father was a wool-grader, came here hoping to do better, make more money, I guess. I can see him, always with his nose in a book."

"Did they have relatives here in the Cotswolds?"

"Not to my knowing. The boys now, there was Cassius and Augustus. Fancy names. We shortened them to Cash and Gus." The old man shook his head as if memories swayed him. "I mind so well."

"My grandfather's name was Augustus."

"They was bonny lads, Cash and Gus. That's what a Scot would say."

"But they left their parents — "

"To go to America. Seems the family came into a little money somehow, enough for passage there, where the boys panted to go. They were young men by that time. How'd they fare?" The old eyes waited her answer with faded interest.

"I know Cassius died a few years after their arrival. Some unidentified disease."

"Like the bloody flux people used to talk about?"

"I don't know. But Augustus, my grandfather, lived for a long time. I remember him well from my girlhood."

"And probably forgot all about home," Mr. Steele said on a note of grievance.

"Not a bit of it, Mr. Steele. He always spoke of the Cotswolds as a heaven of a place. He was planning a visit here when he died suddenly of heart disease."

"Glad to hear that. Not about his dying, I mean."

"Could you tell me where they lived? Is the house still standing?"

"Torn down years ago," he answered. "It was condemned to make way for the new road. That's the way it is. No respect for old things. You might find a picture of it somewhere, but I don't know where."

"I'm grateful for what you have told me."

He might not have heard. "I'm ninety-one years old. That's old enough to forget who you are, who you were, and what's the use anyhow? Change, that's the rule of nature."

"I must say, if you'll excuse me, that you're remarkable."

"Yes, a joy to behold. Say, the church keeps records. You could find the birth dates of the boys there and the names of their parents."

A knock sounded at the door. Mrs. Brownlow entered. She asked brightly, "Is there something I can bring you?"

Mr. Steele stirred and answered, "It's too late and also too early for tea. Isn't that so?"

"I really don't want anything," Geeta said.

"I just thought I'd ask."

Mrs. Brownlow was about to depart when the old man spoke again. "Now hold on. Hold on. Not time for tea, but how about a little drink?" An upheld hand stayed Mrs. Brownlow. "I usually have one about this time. Doctor's orders."

Mrs. Brownlow sniffed.

"How about it, Miss? It's single malt and good for the system."

"If you really would like one."

"Bring it on, Mrs. Brownlow."

Mrs. Brownlow left and returned with a bottle, a pitcher of water, and glasses. "I'll pour for Mr. Steele," she said.

"Now don't you scant me." He turned to Geeta. "She don't trust me with a bottle."

Mrs. Brownlow handed him his glass, then asked Geeta, "Will you pour for yourself?"

"Please."

After Geeta had taken a couple of spoonfuls and added water, Mrs. Brownlow took the bottle and left the room.

Mr. Steele said, "You'd think at my age I could misbehave all I wanted or was capable of, but there's always a woman around to insist on what's good for me. Good for me, hell. What do I care? Why should I care?"

"For the sake of people who care for you," Geeta answered. "They don't want to lose you."

"All right. All right. More woman-talk from you." He took

a small swallow. "I shouldn't complain. Mrs. Brownlow's a good woman."

"That's certainly my impression."

"Now don't you go telling me she means well. People who mean well have done more wrong than God can count. It must tickle Him. God's got a mean sense of humor."

A glint of mischief appeared in the old eyes and as quickly died away.

"Anyhow, you mind what she says, if I dare tell you that."

"Tell me anything. It doesn't matter." He drank the last of his drink and hunched back, putting his uncovered hand back under the robe. He closed his eyes. "Bloody thing to be tired all the time." The words came out in a mutter and ended in a slow whisper.

"I'm ever so grateful, Mr. Steele," Geeta said. "Thanks for seeing me."

Mr. Steele didn't answer. His chest rose and fell to his slow breath.

Geeta tiptoed from the room. At the door she said to Mrs. Brownlow, "I'm so sorry. I tired him out. He went to sleep."

"Now don't you worry. He does that. Just drops off, sometimes in the middle of a sentence."

Geeta said goodbye and thanks and left the house.

The street had come alive — men, women, children, a dog or two, people with smiling faces, people with sober ones, pausing to look in windows or at open displays, taking time to chat, walking on. It was as if householders left their homes just to mingle with others. Some carried small baskets or sacks, as if they shopped every day. Perhaps they had to, buying just a couple of chops or a small portion of cheese or just a vegetable or two because they lacked freezers or refrigerators. Whatever the reason, it made for social gatherings that argued somewhat against the American practice of stocking up.

The church stood down and across the street. Uncertain

whether to visit the vicarage adjacent to the church or the church itself, she entered the latter.

The place was dark and empty except for one woman near the front who seemed to be praying. She looked vaguely familiar. No one answered Geeta's knocks at the side doors.

She retreated and went to the vicarage, where a neat, small, jacketed man, his tie firmly in place, came to the door. "Good morning," he said brightly as he swung it open. "I'm the new vicar, Richard Jackson. Just tell me if I may be of help."

Without entering, she told him her purpose.

"To be sure. To be sure," he answered. "The records room is at one side of the church. Will you come with me?"

In the church the woman was still praying. They went into the side room, where the records lay, pile on pile. "Do you have an idea of the dates?" he asked.

"Not much," she replied. "Somewhere in the eighteen eighties, I would guess."

"The name again, please?"

"Hawthorne."

He consulted an index book. "Oh, yes, yes," he said. "Here it is. Now, just a minute."

With her help he wrestled the volume he wanted from underneath others. "Not such a chore as I feared." He laid the volume on a table. "The first note of Hawthornes in the eighties occurs on page thirty."

She took a note pad and a pencil from her purse and turned to the page. All right, there was Cassius, with birth date and parentage, and ten pages later she found Augustus. They were sons of Julian and Edith Hawthorne, of whom there was no further mention.

"I suppose they left for other parts," the vicar said. He looked at her, sunny-faced, as if glad to have been of assistance.

"You've been very helpful, and I thank you," she said. "Now let me put things back."

"Not to worry. The sexton will do that."

"I'm sorry. I should have asked for him."

"It would not have availed you, I fear," he answered with a smile. "He's on vacation."

Outside, she decided to call on the grocer, Mr. Ebersole, slim though the chances were there. Her route home led past the store. At least she could buy some wine.

The place was packed with fresh fruits and vegetables, canned goods, cookies, and bottles of wine, all tidily arranged.

A small, stooped man without a jacket came to wait on her, his old eyes expectant. His black suspenders contrasted with a white shirt. "Yes, lady," he said.

"I'd like some white wine, dry, and not too expensive."

He nodded. The years had worn tracks in his face, but his eyes were bright. Geeta guessed his age at eighty or almost.

"Of course," he answered. "There's a great deal of nonsense about wines, vintages and all that, but I stock a very good French white wine that's not too expensive."

"And not sweet."

"Assuredly not." He nodded his head at her, as if the two of them knew a thing or two. "It's the uneducated palate that likes wine sweet."

Another customer entered and began examining the vegetables, but the grocer seemed in no hurry. "I hope you're enjoying the Cotswolds," he said.

"Very much, thank you."

He rubbed his hands and nodded his head. "A pleasant country," he said. "Not much given to change. I've lived here a long time, though I'm not a native."

"Is the name Hawthorne familiar to you?"

"Hawthorne? Well, yes, from a long time ago." He half-closed his eyes, trying to recall.

"It was my maiden name, so I'm interested."

"Going back, before I moved here, there was a family named Hawthorne, so I'm told. Man and wife and two sons, as I remember. Scots, they were. When the two sons left home, the old people went back to Scotland. That was the story I picked up."

"They were my people."

Mr. Ebersole smiled benignly. "Fine. Then to go on, there was a lady by the name of Hawthorne who lived in the village for a time. That must be twenty-odd years ago. Hannah Hawthorne. Yes," he went on, agreeing with his memory, "that was her name."

The voice of a customer rose. "Mr. Ebersole, I've got to pay and leave." Even as he called, two more customers entered.

"You'll have to excuse me, please," Mr. Ebersole said. "Coming on to my busy time. Can't we talk later, maybe the middle of the morning sometime, when trade drops off?"

"Surely. I understand," she answered.

Bottle, umbrella, and purse in hand, her bill paid, she left the shop.

Chapter Eight

PERKINS AND GOODMAN were already in the cottage when Charleston entered after breakfast. "All quiet in the incidents room," Perkins said by way of greeting.

"So that's what you call this?"

"That's it. Headquarters for the time being. Place for reports, interviews, phone calls, and deep thinking. Sit down, Mr. Charleston."

Charleston sat, lighted a thin cigar and said through the smoke, "I answer to Chick."

"Fine. Call me Fred then. Tarvin should be here any minute. By the way, the inquest is set for two o'clock tomorrow. You needn't attend. Up to you."

"About this Tarvin, and being in jail."

"Yes, but how long in jail? Did Doggett let him out early, say about midnight or so? Did Doggett remember to lock him in? If he did get out, was Tarvin sober enough to kill a man? A lot of questions." He shifted impatiently. "Where the hell is Doggett? Where's Tarvin?"

As if he had heard him, Doggett opened the door then and let in another man before he entered himself. The man might have been an athlete once. His shoulders were broad and his arms heavy, but his belly bulged over his belt, and the cheeks of his broad face were swollen and drooping. His gaze, though, was direct.

"Good morning," Perkins told him. "Good of you to come in. You're Tarvin? Peter Tarvin? Fine. Won't you sit down?" Perkins motioned to a chair next to Charleston's, and Tarvin took it, breathing short.

"You're a salesman, Mr. Tarvin, and — "

"Sales representative."

"Yes, of course. And you were a guest at the Ram's Head Inn night before last?"

"If you know, why ask me?"

Charleston hadn't expected that from the man.

"Just to be sure," Perkins answered, unaffected. "You know a man was murdered here that night, the twenty-first, or early the next morning?"

"Do I?"

"Don't you?"

"I heard so."

"All right. He was."

"What's that got to do with me?" Tarvin wasn't exactly belligerent, just difficult, Charleston thought. In the rear of the room Goodman was taking notes. Doggett listened with his mouth open.

"I don't know that it has anything to do with you. Maybe no. Maybe yes. That's what we're going to find out."

"The answer is not anything. Not one damn thing."

"You got drunk in the bar at the inn night before last."

"I'm not denying that, nor bragging about it, either."

"You not only got drunk, you got quarrelsome, wanted to fight anyone and everyone."

Tarvin nodded soberly. "That could be."

"You don't remember?"

"Very little. I draw blanks when I drink. But I do get mood

changes from whisky. I know that. And I'll say what you're thinking. I'm a bloody fool to drink if it makes me mean."

Charleston dropped his cigar in a tray.

"Do you remember being jailed?"

"I remember being let out. That's all."

"Who jailed you?"

Tarvin motioned. "I suppose it was the constable here, but I couldn't swear to it."

"It was Doggett all right, but he had help."

"You can't prove it by me."

"His help was Oliver Smith. Ever hear of him?"

"Just now."

"It was Smith who got it. Stabbed through the heart."

"So what?"

"What do you have to say?"

"Just this. If you're trying to fasten that killing on me, that's ridiculous. Who am I, Batman or something, able to fly out a jail window or pass through a locked door? Of all the bloody ideas!"

"But if you don't remember getting drunk and being jailed," Charleston interrupted, "then you wouldn't remember getting up and getting out and stabbing a man, would you?"

"Mister, when I pass out, I pass out. No waking, no moving until I wake up in the morning with a head nobody would believe. Jesus is witness to that."

"He's absent," Perkins answered, making a mouth. "Now, could you have got out of jail once you were put there?"

"Through a locked door?"

"But was the cell locked?" Perkins turned. "Constable Doggett, how about it?"

"I always lock it."

"That doesn't answer the question. Did you lock it after putting Tarvin inside?"

"That's my memory, sir."

"Memory be damned. Are you sure?"

Tarvin interrupted. "I can answer for him. It was the cell door being unlocked that woke me up. It makes a screech." He added, looking around, "Like somebody forgot to oil it. Poor upkeep, I would say."

Charleston smiled inwardly.

"I got no call to use it much, sir," Doggett answered.

Perkins spoke to Charleston. "Any more questions?"

"Maybe just one. Mr. Tarvin, you say you draw blanks when you're drunk. You wouldn't remember then if you did get out of bed, get out of the jail, go to the inn and murder a man. Is that right?"

Tarvin looked Charleston in the eye. "Mister, I tell you this. Without sleeping the drunk off like I did, I couldn't have hit the ground with my hat."

Perkins moved in his chair before saying, "All right, Tarvin. We'll want you to sign a statement that Sergeant Goodman will prepare. Then you may go. But we'll want to know how to get in touch with you, just in case."

Tarvin stood up, searched in his wallet, got out a card, and presented it. "My company knows where I am day to day."

"Thank you."

After Tarvin had signed the statement and let himself out, Charleston said, "He's one independent character."

"Good on the defensive," Perkins said. "Knows how to — what is it? — yes, pass the buck. Wouldn't you say so, Doggett?"

"I say nothin' against him, sir. He spoke up for me."

"So he did." Perkins stretched. "I don't know about you, but I need a breath of fresh air." He stood up and walked out, the others following.

Outside, Perkins drew Charleston away a few steps and said, "We have those first statements of the Americans, as you know. About all we learned was that Smith and Mrs. Post were brother and sister. If there's anything more to be found,

and there damn well must be, we'll have to dig it out. Problem there." He rubbed his chin with one hand. "But I've got an idea. Leave them alone for now. What I'm thinking of is clearing away the underbrush meanwhile, the help and all that. What do you say?"

"Let the foreigners sweat, huh?"

"Something like that was in my mind. It won't hurt them to stew."

Charleston grinned at him. "Shame on you, treating my fellow Americans that way."

"Anything wrong with that?"

"Not a thing in the world. Nice and foxy. Go to it."

Abruptly Charleston put out a restraining hand as Perkins turned to go back inside. "Fred, I'm just wondering. I don't quite know why. Could we talk first to that girl, Rose what's-her-name, who found the body?"

"We've already got her statement."

"It was just a notion."

"What I need is notions," Perkins said and called out, "Sergeant Goodman."

Goodman came up, saying, "Sir?"

"Would you see," Perkins continued, "if it's convenient for Rose Whaley to see us now?"

"Yes, sir."

As Goodman walked away, Perkins said, "I could have told him to fetch her, whether or not, but no. Not me."

They went back into the cottage, leaving the door open at Perkins's suggestion. Doggett followed them. "Stuffy, even outside," Perkins said. Seated, he loaded and lighted his pipe. Outside a dog barked, breaking the morning's stillness, and quit as a man scolded it.

Goodman entered with the girl, saying, "Miss Whaley, sir," and proceeded to his seat in the rear.

"Good morning, Miss Whaley," Perkins said. "I hope we're not interfering too much with your work. Please sit down."

She remained standing, saying, "Not too much yet."

She was full-breasted, blooming with youth, a trifle heavier, perhaps, than she wanted to be. Her face was fresh and quite serious. She wore a maid's uniform.

"Please be seated," Perkins said again. "Do you know my associate, Mr. Charleston?"

The girl sank slowly in the chair. "I've seen him around."

"He'd like to ask you some questions."

"I've already told all I know." Her voice seemed strained, perhaps only the strain of being quizzed.

"Yes," Charleston said, "but perhaps something escaped your memory. Perhaps you recall something that didn't seem important to you but may to us."

"I can't imagine — "

"I understand you found Mr. Smith rather late in the morning?" Charleston asked.

"I've already said so. When I went to make up his room."

"Yes?"

"He was lying there, with a knife sticking out of his back."

"I see. Now how did you happen to go in?"

"I knocked first, like always with our guests, and when there was no answer, I walked in to make up the room."

"You opened the door and went in?"

"I don't see what's wrong with that."

"Nothing. Did you open the door with a key?"

"Making up the rooms, I carry a key, of course."

"But did you use it?"

The girl seemed uncertain. "Well, I — here's what I seem to remember. I started to unlock the door, but it wasn't locked."

Perkins sat quietly, puffing at his pipe.

"When you found the body, what did you do?"

"I ran for help. I shouted."

"You didn't touch him to make sure he was dead?"

"I knew he was dead."

"How could you be sure?"

"Why — why, the knife was sticking in him."

"You didn't enter the room again, not after help came?"

"I've already told Inspector Perkins I didn't. I just couldn't do it."

Charleston asked quietly, "How well did you know Mr. Smith?"

"All these questions," Rose answered, her voice rising. "Questions, more questions, and for what?" Her patience had turned into defiance. "I've told what I know once. It's enough to drive a person crazy. Question. How well did I know Mr. Smith? I knew him as a guest of the inn, like all of us on the staff. Oh, I knew him well enough to say, 'Good morning, Mr. Smith.' Make something out of that."

"Not unless there's something in it, Miss Whaley. What was your impression of him?"

"None. He was just a guest."

"Friendly with the others in his group?"

"Ask them, why don't you?"

"We will, of course. You have a room here at the hotel, do you not?"

"A little bed-sitting room. It's my home."

"Did you hear anything unusual, any noises, any commotion, the night of the murder?"

"No. My room's pretty far away."

With his hand Charleston made a little motion of dismissal. "I believe that's all, Rose, unless Inspector Perkins has more questions?"

Perkins put his pipe aside and shook his head. "You can go back to work, Rose. We're obliged for your help."

The girl left without speaking.

Perkins looked at his watch. "Lunch," he said. "Doggett, hold down the fort until we get back. Goodman, lead us to that pub again."

They walked the two blocks to the pub, through a lunchtime crowd that seemed intent on destination but not worried much about time of arrival. Charleston found he liked this kind of commotion, where people smiled in passing and gave you polite room to pass. A polite people, here in the villages at least, where gregariousness seemed the order of things. Everybody out for lunch. Everybody at once.

The pub sign bore the name Stag and Hind, and underneath was the the notation "Free House." It had a small bar or counter. A tall, bald man stood behind it, unflustered as order after order came to his ears while his hands worked.

Perkins and Goodman ordered ham sandwiches and beer, and Charleston asked for Welsh rarebit and beer.

Sooner than expected, the bartender had their orders ready. With them in hand they turned to find some place to sit. Five tables in the place, Charleston counted, three fully occupied, two only partly so. The men at one of the tables moved over to make room.

Munching on his rarebit, sipping at his beer, Charleston compared customs. No waiters in a pub, not like in America. You waited on yourself here. And people expected to share tables and did so with smiles. Better spirit than offishness. The rarebit was excellent.

He asked Goodman, seated next to him, "What's a free house?"

"One not owned by some corporation that limits the brands on sale to those it makes or handles. Independent is what it means."

The customers at their table stood up and went out, and before any others arrived, Perkins asked Charleston, "What about Rose? Anything there, you think?"

"Maybe."

"You rather laid into her, didn't you, Chick?"

"I guess I did. I wanted to shake her up and succeeded there at least. Maybe to some purpose."

"Who's up this afternoon, Sergeant?"

Two other customers took seats at their table, both full of talk, not listening to Goodman's answer.

"The night man. I woke him up. He's one. Then that bus boy, Larry Bates, and the bellman. I have his name in my notes. Mrs. Vaughn, if you want her. There's a gardener, too, that I managed to locate. The other waitress, name of Betty Saunders. I doubt you're interested in the new chef, but the old cook's around helping in the kitchen. The bartender, too, a young woman. There's a dishwasher and kind of daily woman. Not in, but she'll be around later. That sounds like a full afternoon, but someone around here has to know something." He shook his head. "That's for us to find out, and by God we will."

They gulped the last of their beers and walked back to the cottage.

The telephone was ringing as they entered. Doggett took the call, said, "For you," to Perkins, and added, "Got to go. Got a complaint." He hurried out.

"Yes," Perkins was saying. "All right." His hand reached over for pencil and note pad. "Give it to me." He scribbled for a while, then sat down, loaded his pipe, and fired up. "That was headquarters," he said between puffs. "Autopsy report. We were right about the time. Midnight, or within about an hour either way. Smith was in excellent shape, except for the knife that killed him. No other signs of violence. No evidence of poison. Nothing on fingerprints. He had had sex or at least an ejaculation some time before he was stabbed."

"Reward and punishment," Goodman said wryly.

"If you're going to get religious on me, make it sin and atonement," Perkins said. "And by the way, the super is coming tomorrow."

"Blessed day," the sergeant intoned.

"Well, time to get to work. Sit down, Chick. Who's up, Sergeant Goodman?"

"Whoever you want."

"Make it the night man then."

While Goodman was gone, Charleston said, "Nothing on the knife?"

"It went to Gloucester for examination, along with the body and what other little evidence there was. Horn-handled. No prints on it."

"You've traced it?"

"Oh, sorry. It's a mate to one in the kitchen. Identical. Suggests an inside job, eh?"

Charleston didn't have to answer, for the door opened then to admit Goodman and an older man, a lot older, Charleston saw on second glance. He wore a pair of worn trousers and a half-buttoned shirt, both wrinkled as if he had slept in them, as Charleston supposed he might have.

"Have a chair, sir," Perkins said, "and give me your name if you will." He put his pipe on the desk.

The man sat down, his eyes rolling suspiciously from Perkins to Charleston and back. His toothless mouth opened to say, "Harold Opey, just Ope to most folk."

"We know you're the night man. You answer the bell if anyone comes in late. Right?"

"Mostly I hear it first ring."

"Does that happen often?"

"Just once lately. That was Mr. Smith, him that got himself killed. Smelled of strong drink, he did, and pushed past me like I hadn't put myself out to let him in. Uncivil, I'd say."

"Was that your only encounter with him?"

"Once was enough."

"Do you know, were the other doors locked, the side and back doors?"

"Mrs. Vaughn or somebody sees to that. Not my business."

"Did you notice anything unusual the night of the murder? Unusual sounds? Noises? Footsteps? Voices? Anything?"

"There wasn't none, and I sleep light."

Perkins glanced at Charleston, who gave him a shake of the

head. "That's all, Mr. Opey," he said. "We appreciate your cooperation."

"All, eh?" Opey answered as if he couldn't believe it. At Perkins's nod he let himself out the door.

"Mrs. Vaughn next?" Charleston asked. "I'd feel better with a doctor present. She's frail as a potato chip."

Perkins smiled. "I guess you mean what we call a crisp."

Goodman raised a questioning eye. "Mrs. Vaughn?"

"No. Not now, anyhow," Perkins answered. "You know, Sergeant, we've already questioned her at length, and all we got out of it was a collapse or damn near it. Let's tackle the bus boy. Larry Bates, isn't it?"

Goodman went out the door, to return in no more than five minutes. While he was gone, Charleston said, "That bus boy's big enough to eat hay."

"Strong as a horse, too, by the looks of him. Good at all sports, I hear. Keeps in condition." Perkins fired up his pipe and took a couple of quick puffs before setting it down again.

Larry Bates looked around on entering, then took his seat. The sleeves of his tan shirt were rolled up and showed the fine hair of early manhood. Later it would thicken and coarsen, and he could call himself Tarzan, a name that his build already suggested. His manner seemed defensive, a not unusual attitude for strangers to police questioning. Asked if he had heard anything out of the ordinary on the night of the murder, he answered, "How could I? When I get through work, I go home. That's about ten-thirty, sometimes a little later."

"Home?" Perkins continues.

"Home to my mum's. That's where."

"What about Mr. Smith? Had you seen him enough to form an opinion?"

The boy's jaw tightened. His voice strengthened. "I seen him enough, all I wanted to and more."

Perkins asked, "Why was that?"

"Treated us help like dogs, he did." He swallowed his
anger, thought a second, and added, "His own folks didn't
have any time for him."

"They didn't?"

"Only Mr. Witt, he put up with him, and Mrs. Post, she
gave him some notice. But not Mr. Post, no, sir. It was like he
got mad just seeing him."

"Now, Larry, was the place locked up the night of the
murder, side door and back? Did you attend to that?"

"Sometimes I do. Sometimes I don't. Depends."

"On what?"

"Mrs. Vaughn. Half the time she does it."

"But what about that night?"

"Best I remember, we kind of did it together. All you have
to do is put the lock on self-lock, so it catches tight when the
door is closed from outside."

"And you did it together?"

"I think so. I was quitting work, and she just kind of went
along, being friendly."

Bates was dismissed then, and more staff members called.
Witnesses came, spoke, and departed. The bellman was a
scrawny kid whose face fell into retreat below his nose, leaving
a pout of a mouth and a button for a chin. All he knew about
Mr. Smith was he didn't throw his money around. The gardener, Joseph Jones, an old man, knew nothing at all. Betty
Saunders, the second waitress, was no help, except Mr. Smith
was bloody gruff and close with his money. Nothing from the
old cook, who was assisting the new chef, and nothing from the
dishwasher, a stout village woman, who tried hard to dig up
information but couldn't find any.

Perkins had hoped for more from the young bar woman,
Janie Rogers. She came in demurely, a fair-haired girl of
perhaps twenty-two, dressed in a simple flowered dress. She
took the seat indicated and said, "Yes, sir."

After she had given her name, Perkins asked, "You were

on duty last Monday night, the night the fight took place in the bar?"

"Yes, sir, I was. I work just part time and that was one of the nights."

"Tell us about the fight."

"I'm sorry. I guess it was my fault, but until he got quarrelsome, the man didn't show any signs of having too much to drink. It came on all of a sudden."

"What was it about?"

"Oh, Lordy, who knows? You know how drunks are."

"Not altogether, miss. How did the man Tarvin come to brace Mr. Smith?"

"I don't know, unless it was that Mr. Smith tried to calm him down when he began swearing. Right afterwards Constable Doggett came in."

"And Tarvin objected to being thrown out?"

"He sure did, but he wasn't making any sense."

"Did he threaten Mr. Smith?"

"Not that I heard. He was just swearing and shouting and then he went limp."

Perkins dismissed her.

After she left, Perkins shrugged, blew out a long plume of smoke, and said, "So much for the underbrush. Damn little there."

Goodman said, "There's still Mrs. Vaughn."

"We'll get to her tomorrow, her and the Americans again. Oh, hell, there's the inquest then. Always some bloody thing getting in the way of work."

"Yes, sir, like dinner. You must be hungry."

"You mean *you* are. You're always hungry, Sergeant."

"Yes, sir. And thirsty now in the bargain."

"All right. Until tomorrow. Bright and early, then, to catch the goddamn worm. Doggett's nosing around. At least I asked him to. He may come up with something."

"That's sure looking on the bright side."

*

Over dinner that night, Geeta asked, "Do you have to spend so much time on this case?"

"I do, Geeta, and you know why. I can't sit by and let a good man go down. Besides that, not so important, though, I'd like to show up that joker of a superintendent."

"They're certainly making use of you while you're here."

"Time's short. Mine is."

"Did you notice the Posts and Witts are here tonight?"

"Along with what seems to be a new batch of tourists."

"And another thing, Chick. Did you notice that the waitress, Rose you call her, didn't speak to us when she came for our order?"

"That's my doing. She got upset at some of my questions."

She shook her head, stopped, and shook it again. "What a mess!"

"Forget it, for now anyhow. You haven't told me about your day."

"What about my day is that I've missed the bus."

"How's that?"

"The older Hawthornes, you know, my great-grandfather, moved to the Cotswolds from Scotland and went back there after the boys had sailed for America. Moved back, of all places, to Fort William or near there." She added with disgust, "And we were just there."

"Spilled milk," Charleston told her.

"Oh, all right, but I'm not quite crying over it. I've got a lead on a woman named Hawthorne who lived here for a while. She might have been a relative. A nice grocer told me about her, then got too busy to talk. I'll know more shortly. Tell you about it later on. Come along. Forget your darned case and come. We can have coffee in the lobby."

Chapter Nine

CHARLESTON WAS DRESSING the next morning when the telephone rang. "Morning, Chick," the voice said. "Perkins here."

"Hi, Fred."

"I called to tell you Superintendent Hawley is here." Charleston gathered from his tone that Hawley was in the room with him. "With him are the pathologist, the coroner, and a detective constable he thinks we may need."

"Yes."

"Superintendent Hawley wants to go over our reports this morning. The inquest is this afternoon. There are witnesses to be notified and jurors to be summoned."

"You're telling me to stay put?"

"Not quite that. I just don't want you to waste your time. I thought I'd save you that."

"Thanks, Fred. No reason for me not to attend the inquest?"

"None at all. See you there."

"Red-tape delay, Geeta," Charleston said after he had hung up. "Nothing for me until the inquest, if then. That's what Perkins said, but I have other ideas."

"What?"

"I've heard mention of a Mr. Vaughn. I aim to call on him."

"Just so it's not dangerous."

"Not even close."

"Let's hurry. I want coffee."

She ate a light breakfast, just juice, toast, and coffee, and at the end put a napkin to her lips and stood up. "I'm going to follow the one lead I have, you know, with the grocer, and then maybe go antiquing."

"You go ahead then." He looked at his watch. "Too early to go visiting."

He ordered more coffee when she had gone and sipped at it, willing the time to pass, wishing the minutes away until a decent hour for a visit arrived.

The coffee finished, he walked into the lobby. A woman he hadn't seen before was at the desk. Out of habit he asked if there was any mail for him and then said, "Oh, sorry. My name's Charleston."

"Yes," she answered, smiling. "I know that." She looked at the mail slots and added, "Nothing today."

"Fair's fair," he said, returning her smile. "If you know my name, it's due me to hear yours."

"I'm Jane Witherspoon. I lease a cottage in back of the inn and help out here when I can. I've known Mrs. Vaughn for years."

She wore a white blouse, rather frilly and altogether feminine. In contrast, her dark hair, beginning to show streaks of gray, was drawn severely back from her face. But the face was friendly and quick to smile.

"It seems we've neglected you," he said.

"How?"

"A sad case of discrimination." He grinned into the friendly eyes. "All the rest of the staff have been questioned."

"Oh, I'm a murder suspect?"

"I wouldn't use that word. Were you here the night of the murder?"

"In my cottage. I'm not steady help, Mr. Charleston. Just

during the season and at other times if Mrs. Vaughn wants me. I fill in at the desk and help Rose sometimes with the rooms. You know Rose? Oh, but never mind, Mr. Charleston. I know you have things to do."

He consulted his watch. "Not quite yet. Yes, I know Rose, the waitress."

"Also the maid." The woman glanced around the vacant lobby, then leaned forward, resting her elbows on the counter, "I tell you that girl has her hands full, even with the help of the bus boy. You've seen him? Larry Bates?"

"Yes."

"They get along so well, those two. One day we'll hear wedding bells, I imagine." She smiled at the thought. Then the smile faded as she added, "That girl takes too much on herself. Every afternoon she goes to see Mr. Vaughn."

"Every day?"

"Yes indeed, or almost. He's a cripple and doesn't often leave the house."

"Rose sounds overdedicated to duty."

"Overdedicated to kin is more like it. But goodness, you don't want to waste time talking to me."

He smiled. "Kin, you said?"

"Rose is Mrs. Vaughn's niece, the daughter of her older sister, who's been dead for years. Died when Rose was six years old. So Mrs. Vaughn took her to raise. The father, a Cockney, was no good and glad to get rid of the child. Pity."

"Never seen since?"

"Never."

The outer door opened, and Mrs. Vaughn came in. She put her hat on a rack and went behind the counter, smiling.

"Thank you, Jane," she said. Then, to both of them, "It's a grand morning, a good day for a walk. I'd have gone farther if I could, the church is so close." She was still panting a little. "You two getting acquainted?"

"Pleasantly," Charleston answered. "Nothing to do this

morning, and I'm thinking of taking a stroll myself, just chatting with people. Your husband, Mrs. Vaughn? What about him? Would he mind passing the time of day?"

"He'd welcome it, but the house is hardly far enough away for a real walk. It's just one street over" — she pointed — "and two streets up, on the corner. You'll notice the flowers, a lot of primroses."

"Maybe I'll go then."

"Shall I call him for you and ask him?"

"I don't want to push."

"Nonsense." She lifted the phone from the desk behind her, dialed, spoke, and came back. "He'll be delighted," she said.

He had no difficulty in finding the house. In front of it primroses of all hues marched, curved, straightened out and marched back, all in order, all, it seemed, in step, each carrying its own blooming guidon. That was the thing about flower gardens in England. They were disciplined, formal, each shaped as if to the demands of a blueprint — which maybe they actually were. And the flowers in this climate bloomed and bloomed in a way to astonish a Montanan. Lucky back home to grow a few petunias.

He knocked on the door and waited and presently heard halting steps. The door opened. In the doorway stood a man with a cane in his hand. He wore an open yellow shirt, brown trousers, and bedroom slippers. His face was checked and seamed like a dried mud flat.

"Good morning, Mr. Vaughn," Charleston said. "I'm the man your wife called you about. Charleston's the name." He held out his hand. "I've come a-visiting."

Vaughn took the hand in a gnarled one. "Bullshit! You're an American law officer, and I'm a suspect. Come in, damn it, come in. You talk like an American."

"And you don't?"

"I'm a bit contaminated from hearing you Yanks."

Vaughn turned unsteadily, feeling with his cane. He led the way into a small sitting room. "Take a seat." With one hand on a chair arm and his stick in the other, he did so himself. Once down, he took a puffing breath. "How's the murder scene?"

"Cloudy," Charleston answered. He lowered himself into a chair.

"So you're raking field and stream, huh? Count me out. I'm hors de combat."

"But you're able to move about?"

"You know I am, if you remember. I was in the lobby when you checked in at the inn."

"I remember."

"It's just on good days I hobble down to the inn. They come once in a while, not often enough. But I manage to care for my flowers. Doesn't take much time or effort."

"There's just one word for your garden. Beautiful."

"Thanks. Mostly I just sit around and cuss the luck."

"That help?" Charleston smiled as he asked.

Vaughn smiled in return and gave a small, rueful shake of his head. "Doesn't hurt, and it lets off steam. Oh, I get along. There's Rose. She's damn near a daughter, and she comes every day and knocks up the place, and maybe cooks a little something for me to eat later. A good girl, Rose. You know her?"

"Oh, yes."

"Worries me sometimes. You know, it's a sad fact, but she's maybe not too bright in the head. She's gentle and good-intentioned and not hard to look at. And you might say at her age she's ripe." Vaughn shook his head. "Some day some bloke will get to her, and there'll be all hell to pay. I wouldn't like it, of course, but my wife, now! When she learns, she'll be fit to be tied. One big blow-up. Got her own ideas about morals. Old-fashioned from heaven. God's right above us with his eye peeled. Smiles on the righteous, and to burning hell with the sinners. A true believer, that's Helen."

"You're not so devout?"

Vaughn laughed without mirth. The laugh added wrinkles to his face. "Devout? Jesus! Who's devout with a pain in his arse, not to mention hands, legs, and backbone? No, I'm not devout. I got a thing or two to say to God if ever I meet the bastard." He sighed then, the laugh gone. "Oh, well, hell. There's no sense in fighting over religion. It seems to help my wife. She's not very well. And I keep my mouth closed."

Charleston nodded.

"Like I was saying, I get along." He paused as if thinking about getting along. "My wife pops around whenever she can and once a week spends the night. I'm not so old or crippled that I don't like a woman in my bed. I can click all right, but I have to be careful."

"That's something."

"And my wife doesn't seem to mind," Vaughn went on as if he so seldom had visitors that he didn't balk at intimacies. "I don't know as she gets any joy out of it, but she accepts me for what I am."

He continued, his voice touched with sadness now, "She lost a lot of vitality and spirit after a heart attack a year ago. She's not like her old self. Now everything seems to fuss her. I don't know how long she can go on managing the inn. She has good help from Mrs. Witherspoon, of course, and Constable Doggett is always on call in case of trouble. But I don't know about that joker. He's so bloody stupid. He wouldn't know he had walked in shit unless someone told him so."

Charleston thought to change the subject by asking, "What did you do before you retired?"

"I was in wool. A broker. Bought and sold and made money. Business was good in those days, and I put enough aside to buy the inn. Lucky thing I did. That was before taxes got so high a man couldn't save sixpence. Goddamn greedy government. But what about yourself? You haven't said more'n a word. No chance to, with me rattling on." His pouched eyes were inquiring. "Where's home?"

"In the state of Montana, U.S.A."

"Montana?"

"Interior northwest of America, against the Canadian border."

"Married?"

"Yep. Very happily."

"Children?"

"No. Hopeless, it seems."

"Too bad. Maybe for the best. Who knows. And now you're helping our little boys with the batons?"

"I'm not sure. Make it I'm trying to."

"Say, how about a drink?"

"Thanks. Too early for me. I have to be going, anyhow. Now, don't get up."

Mr. Vaughn stood up regardless. He put a hand on Charleston's shoulder. "Come back. Hear me? I don't mind being a suspect, so come again."

Out on the main street, Charleston looked at his watch. He had time enough, if none to spare, and ahead was the chemist's shop. He made for it. The town had wakened up to the noon hour. There was movement on the streets, bustle at the crossings, people in the stores. He went into the chemist's. A small man was attending to one customer, another stood waiting. When they had what they wanted, the little man asked, "Help you, sir?"

He was, in country terms, the spittin' image of Walter Witt, even to the eyeglasses. Take away his occupational apron, put a business suit on him, and there was the exact double.

"A package of razor blades, Swords," Charleston told him.

"Right here, sir. Anything else?"

"That's all." Charleston held out a five-pound note and, as the man made change, said, "I believe I'm acquainted with your brother."

The man smiled. "Old Ponzi. Quite a character. We're twins, you know. Here's your change."

"You could pass for each other."

"I know. He's an operator. Where did you meet him?"

"At the Ram's Head Inn. We're both lodgers."

The man's expression changed from amiability to concern. "I know now. You're the American investigator." The eyes widened. "But he can't be in trouble?"

"At this point everyone is suspect."

"I understand that, but you're barking up the wrong tree there." He added as an afterthought, "Terrible thing, that knife murder."

"No disagreement there."

Witt excused himself to wait on a customer and on his return said, "All we get is rumor. Nothing for sure. Tight-lipped, you police are."

"You'll hear when the time comes."

"Humph. If ever."

"Not too long, we hope. Your brother's evidence is of no help, so far as we can see now."

Witt pulled in a breath. "He couldn't be guilty. I swear to that. We're identical twins. Just like one person in a way. Feel the same impulses, have the same potentials, the same restraints."

Charleston's thoughts dodged back to his first conversation with Mrs. Witt. Twins? "Closer in a sense than man and wife." So she had said. An interesting observation, considering . . .

"I'm glad to have your opinion, Mr. Witt. What do you know about your brother's companions? Or the late Mr. Smith?"

"I never met any of them before, except Walter's wife. She's all right."

"You met the rest after they came here then?"

"Only that Mr. Post. Ben's his name."

"What about him?"

"Nothing. I didn't take to him."

Again a customer interrupted their conversation. When he had gone, Charleston said, "You spoke of your brother as Ponzi?"

"Oh, you know. Full of business. How to make money.

That's him. I didn't mean he was a con man like old Ponzi you still hear about in America. He's an operator, maybe a business genius. Wants me to sell out and go with him to South America. He has interests here and yonder."

"A financier?"

"I suppose. But I don't know about throwing in with him. Got a nice little business and a home right here, so maybe I say no. Depends. Won't hurt him to wait."

Charleston nodded, said, "Thanks for the blades," and turned away. A fourth customer, the fifth counting himself, was entering the shop as he went out. Nice little business, all right.

Chapter Ten

He walked to the Stag and Hind, noting on the way that time had slipped up on him. Traffic on the walks had slowed. There were fewer cars on the street. Women were making last-minute purchases. Two old women, one with a cane, poked along, enjoying the sun.

Old women with canes. He kept seeing them. It was as if, in spite of gimpy legs and perhaps laboring lungs, they would join the crowds or else. Else what? Molder in their lodgings, alone. Well, cheers for them. Go to it, grandmas.

The noontime trade at the pub had thinned. The bald man behind the counter waited on his order. Charleston looked at what was offered. The man said, "Bangers good today, sir, but they're always good, come to that."

"What's the difference between a banger and an ordinary sausage?"

"Aw," the man said, expanding. "It's the difference between a prime piece of meat and a so-so one. Bangers and mash, meaning mashed potatoes, sir, is almost as standard as fish and chips."

"That's for me, then, and thanks."

"Inquest today, so I hear. And will you have a pint with your lunch, sir?"

Charleston took the plate and the pint to a table and proceeded to eat, watching the time as he did so.

The inquest, he had learned, was to be held in the town hall, a two-story building two intersections up from the pub. It contained, he'd been told, a courtroom of sorts for the hearing of minor cases. He stood on the street for a moment, watching the people, the moving cars. The air was just chill enough to be bracing. The sky shone clear with one wandering cloud in it, but it was not the deep, wide, forever sky of Montana. Be thankful anyhow, he told himself.

At five minutes before two o'clock, he entered the hall, climbed the steps to the courtroom and walked in. The coroner was just seating himself. Below him at the side the jurors sat waiting. At a glance he saw in the front row Perkins and Hawley and, presumably, the witnesses. Among them were Rose, Mrs. Vaughn, Mrs. Post, Constable Doggett, and a professional-looking man he took for the pathologist.

The coroner, a round man with a round face and a patient air, called for order as Charleston seated himself. Along with him perhaps a dozen of the curious, mostly men, waited.

Perkins ushered Mrs. Post to the witness stand, where she sat imperturbable. She wore a dark, tailored suit that an admiral might have admired. After she had given her name, the coroner asked, "You were a sister of the deceased?"

"I was."

"And have you identified the body?"

"I have." She barely opened her mouth as she spoke, as if taking care not to squander words.

"Identified it beyond any doubt?"

"Beyond any doubt."

"Identified him as whom?"

"My brother. Oliver C. Smith."

"That's the full name?"

"No. Oliver Cromwell Smith."

A look of astonishment came on the round face. He said, "Really?" as if not expecting an answer. Then, "That's all, Mrs. Post, thank you."

He paused a minute, gazing down at a paper before him, while the jurors, Charleston supposed, chewed over the fact that a man's given name could be Oliver Cromwell. If there were Irishmen in the box, they would be glad he was dead.

The coroner sighed and looked up. Perkins steered the stranger to the stand.

"Your name?" the coroner asked.

"Justin Godwin."

"Your business or profession?"

"I'm a qualified pathologist. In the profession for years."

"I have no doubt of that, sir, but we have just your word."

Perkins stood up. "If you'll excuse me, sir. Dr. Godwin is well known to us in the C.I.D. He is our criminal pathologist, and his credentials are impressive."

"So be it, then. Now, Dr. Godwin, what can you tell us about the death of Mr. Smith, the deceased?"

"He died of a stab wound in the heart. No other signs of injury or abuse. At the time of the stabbing he was in good health. I would say he was in early middle age."

"And what else, Doctor?"

"He had engaged in sex recently, or at any rate had ejaculated."

"And the stab wound. What was its location precisely?"

"Not to be technical about it, it was in the left back toward the side, over the heart."

"Did you draw any conclusions from its location?"

"None except that the wound was fatal."

"Nothing more?"

"I'm not fond of guesses." A smile touched the pathologist's mouth.

"Could the wound have been inflicted during an embrace, say a woman's embrace?"

"I wouldn't venture a conjecture." The doctor might have been tempted to grin.

"We have the evidence of semen."

"No question about that."

"And Smith was found lying dead in bed."

"So I've been told."

Someone near Charleston broke out in a suppressed giggle. Next to him a man with a rabbit's face said loud enough to be heard, "Now we're gettin' to it." Sex had upstaged murder.

"But you have no conjectures, Doctor?" the coroner persisted.

"None. No theories."

"Can you give us the time of the deceased's death?"

"The indications are that he died about midnight on April 21. But allow an hour or so either way."

"I do believe that's all, Dr. Godwin. Thank you. You may step down."

Perkins showed Rose to the stand then, and after her Constable Doggett and Mrs. Vaughn. Rose had on a flowered dress that might have been a trifle big, but not big enough to conceal the young, proud swell of her bosom. She seemed somewhat uneasy but spoke in a firm voice and repeated what she had said to earlier questioning. Doggett in his adenoidal voice said nothing new. Mrs. Vaughn alarmed the coroner. She took the stand unsteadily, her breath short and audible. The twitch of a muscle distorted her mouth. Her voice trembled when she said who she was. She had always reminded Charleston of a wren and now a wren in distress.

The coroner held up his hand and stayed his questions, his face kind and concerned. "Mrs. Vaughn?" he said softly. "Please don't be upset or alarmed. This is a simple hearing, calling for simple answers. Would you like a glass of water? No? Just be at ease then. Take your time. It might help you to breathe deep."

She got through finally, and Perkins himself took the stand and told what he knew.

"Your investigation has been going on since April 22, is that right?" the coroner asked.

"Yes, sir."

"And you are no farther along than in the beginning?"

Perkins turned to stare at him and took time in answering. "I wouldn't say that, and, sir, I don't care for the implications of your question."

The coroner leaned forward and pointed a finger. "I wasn't implying anything, Inspector. You're inferring from what, I'll confess, was a poor choice of words. You haven't determined the identity of the murderer? That's the question."

"No, sir."

"Are there more witnesses?"

"No, sir."

"To sum up," the coroner said, looking toward the jurors, "that's all that is known to date. A man has been killed, murdered apparently. No solution so far, but it's early days yet. This hearing is postponed for ten days."

Superintendent Hawley set a brisk pace back to the incidents room, hardly pausing to introduce the new detective constable to Charleston. The man's name was Rendell. He had alert eyes and a wide mouth that a brief smile spread.

In the incidents room, Hawley, in Perkins's chair, leaned forward to say, "So you've been fishing in the shallows and haven't a minnow to show for it. It's time for the deep waters, wouldn't you say, Inspector?"

"I suppose."

"And you, Mr. Sheriff?"

"We may have netted a minnow or two."

"Show me one."

"In time, Mr. Superintendent, in time. I won't burden you with conjecture."

"Good. No half-baked ideas." Hawley turned away with an almost audible snort. "We'll try the Americans again, Perkins. Who's next? Who's first?"

From the rear Goodman spoke. "I think they're ready. I asked them to be."

"I suggest Mr. Post," Perkins said.

"Bring him in."

Goodman left to get him.

While they waited, Hawley said, "Coroner Jenkins has a cute mind. Right?" He was asking Charleston.

"Cute? Not stupid by a long shot."

"And maybe he has something. Cherchez la femme, eh?"

Perkins interrupted. "Cherchez everybody at this point."

Goodman came in with Post, who grabbed at the chair indicated and sat down with a thump. "It's a temptation to tell you birds to go screw yourselves."

Perkins said, "I wouldn't advise it."

Hawley smiled his tight smile. It didn't touch those shallow gray eyes. Windows of the soul, huh? If so, the shades were drawn. Hawley said, "There's such a thing as obstructing justice."

"Pardon me if my guts shake, I'm laughing so hard. How obstruct it? I don't know anything."

Goodman was taking notes. Doggett and Rendell sat still.

"Then you'll be glad to cooperate," Hawley said, his words a denial of their meaning. "What can you tell us about Oliver C. Smith?"

"Not one damn thing that will help you. But still you keep me on the hook. 'Don't leave, Mr. Post,' you bastards say. 'We'll tell you when you're free. Just stay put, like a good man.' Goddamn, I should have been out of this burg before now."

"That's one thing you've almost told us. That you didn't like him."

"Is there a law saying I have to?"

"He was your brother-in-law."

"Christ sake! I didn't pick him." Post made a sweeping gesture with one hand, dismissing the relationship.

"Did you dislike him enough to kill him?"

"Whoa, now. I'm not that crazy. But if I did hate him enough, somebody beat me to it."

"What brought you to England, Mr. Post?"

"Public transportation. Quite good in this country. Tried it lately?"

Hawley's tone was mean. "Forget the smart-aleck act. Answer the question."

"Beg your pardon all to hell. I came with my business partner, Mr. Witt. He wanted to visit his twin brother."

"That's all?"

"Shut up if you want to hear. No, it's not all. Like her brother, my wife was born in the Cotswolds. Wanted to see the country again. Been a long, long time. Smith, that bastard, was born here, like I said. He came on some business deal. He never told me what."

"Where were you the night of the killing?"

"I answered that once. Don't you birds ever look at your records? I signed a statement saying I was in my room with my wife. Look in the files, for God's sake."

Hawley said, "You seem opposed to our investigation. Why is that?"

"I'm tired of foolishness. I'm tired of cops."

"But you must want us to find the murderer?"

"You say so. I don't."

"It's not too hard to think you're it."

"Think all you please."

"There must be reasons why you hated Oliver Smith. Tell us."

"Tell you nothing. It's personal and none of your business. I didn't stick a knife in his back. You want more from me, see my lawyers in London. That's Clayton, Clayton and Burroughs."

Hawley turned away from him. "Any questions? Perkins? Charleston?"

"Not much to the point, I'm afraid," Charleston said, "but I'm wondering why both Mr. Post and Mr. Smith shaved off their beards?"

Post said, "Well, I'll be goddamned!"

"True, Mr. Post?" Hawley asked.

"Talk about nosy Parkers. You want to know my toilet habits, too? I just got tired of whiskers."

"Smith also?"

"You can ask him. Maybe he kept a diary."

Hawley took a deep breath and let it out in a long sigh. "I can't see that the question of beards is either here or there. All right for now. I'm going to let you go, Mr. Post. For the time being, you understand. Keep yourself within reach."

"Yeah, stick around, stick around, when I ought to be on my way." Post shook his head in disgust. "I'm here too long as it is. Delay. Delay. Shit!"

As Post went out, the phone rang. Perkins moved to take the call, but Hawley struck down his hand, grabbed the receiver and said, "Hawley here." He listened for a moment, hung up with a slam and announced, "More bloody trouble! Headquarters. One goddamn thing, then another. Be back when I can." He got up without another word, strode out, and left the door open.

Over a late dinner with Geeta in the dining room, Charleston said, "I'm sorry about your day, Mr. Ebersole not in the store and all."

"I'll see him tomorrow, I hope. He's not sick, as I said. At his age he just takes a day off now and then."

"And nothing in the antique shops?"

"One beautiful piece of flow-blue. A big platter, oval, perhaps fifteen inches long. Argyle pattern. But oh my! Seventy-five pounds! Too much money, and too big a risk carrying."

"It's too bad, not to find more flow-blue, since you like it so much."

"I saw a Hepplewhite sideboard and a Queen Anne low-boy, both priced at a fortune." She smiled into his eyes. "Anyhow, they were too heavy to carry, even for you."

"Queen Anne, that bow-legged stuff."

She ignored him. "Later on I had tea with Mr. and Mrs. Witt. There was quite a crowd. More tourists as you can see when you look around. The Witts are friendly enough, and I tend to like them." She added with mischief, "Not because Mrs. Witt was born in Glendive, Montana."

He answered in the same spirit. "It should. We're as good as kin."

"Mr. and Mrs. Post, now, they're plainly offish, as if we were tainted. I have a feeling they're not on such good terms with the Witts, either."

"Any examples?"

"No. It's just a feeling." She went silent, scanning his face. "Why don't you knock off tomorrow?"

"We're set to interview Mrs. Post and the Witts."

"And you have to be there."

"Time's so short."

"I know. I know. And you have to solve the case, even if all by yourself." She looked into his eyes and went on, "Chick, you silly man. I adore you."

Chapter Eleven

PERKINS RATHER LOOKED FORWARD to the day as he walked to the inn for breakfast. Now they'd get to the Americans, really get down to business this time. They were bound to know more than they'd said. He'd let Charleston do the questioning, subject to his own interruptions, of course.

Last night he'd gone to the Ram's Head bar for a late drink, for a soothing touch of Morangie with a bit of water. There were six or eight customers in the place, Americans by the sound of them. Until he turned around with the drink in his hand, he did not see Mrs. Witt, seated alone in the rear of the room. She caught his eye and made a small, beckoning gesture. She said, after he had seated himself, "You always look so serious, like a general about to order a charge."

"Murder's a serious business." He let himself smile. She was a pretty thing.

"I would guess you were a soldier once?"

"Ancient history."

She answered lightly, "I can see you're terribly superannuated."

"Quite."

Her face went serious. "Is it fair to ask if you are making progress?"

"Of course. It's also fair to say we are proceeding. Wouldn't you like another drink? Sherry, isn't it?"

"Thanks, no. One's enough." Her teeth were white. She reached out and touched his sleeve, as if to draw his especial attention, then quickly withdrew her hand. "I may have something to tell you."

"Then you'd better tell me, Mrs. Witt. It's not the thing to withhold evidence."

"I don't intend to withhold it." Her eyes were on him. He thought he saw deep, past iris and pupil, deep into a sort of innocent suffering. It had been a long time since he'd been with a woman, let alone a small and fetching one, the kind a man wanted to cuddle, thinking of proud breasts and satin flanks.

He shook the picture from his head. Goddamn it all, he had a career to think about, he subscribed to a code of conduct, as became an officer. And here he was, letting his imagination run like a teen-ager.

She went on, "I'll tell you, of course, but not here. Not now."

"Then tomorrow, when we'll be questioning you."

"Not then, either, but I will tell you. I promise." Her eyes were smiling.

She stood up abruptly, bringing him to his feet to see her off. Like a fool, he held out his hand. She took it, and he felt the pressure and warmth of her.

"I must leave," she said, hesitating. "My husband may have finished one of those interminable chess games he plays with Mr. Post. I pass my nights reading."

"And drinking sherry?"

"Shame on you. Just once in a while, if that interests you."

He might have answered that everything about her interested him. "Won't you sit down again and have another sherry?"

"Not tonight. Thanks."

He found himself saying, "Another time, then?"

She answered, "I hope so," smiled a goodbye, and walked out, her small bottom moving under her trim slacks.

He watched her until she was gone from sight. So long, so long and never with a woman who tugged at his senses like this one. He hoped never to see her alone. Or did he? Put it on the line, get it out in front — did he? The bloody truth, say it! What he wanted and what reason told him were two different things. Better decide in favor of the brain, you fool. Better behave like a good officer. Why had he ever decided to be a policeman? He wasn't cut out for it.

Now, reaching the entrance to the inn, he put last night out of his mind. He saw the Charlestons at a table in the dining room, and, on invitation, joined them. Chick introduced her. She had a serene face and honest and inquiring eyes. Her hair, brushed back from her forehead, was a little longer than was the fashion. She wore a tweed skirt and light, tan jacket over a white blouse with a gold bar pin at the throat. It was his day, Perkins thought, to meet attractive women.

Charleston asked, "Where's the sergeant?"

"Working, I'll wager. You wouldn't ask if you knew Goodman. Up early and away to the incidents room and the typewriter."

Perkins ordered a full English breakfast, ham and eggs, slices of tomato, and toast, with coffee later.

"Chick," he said while he waited, "we've hesitated about questioning Mrs. Vaughn." He lowered his voice, thinking he might have been speaking loud enough for others to hear. "But we can't overlook her."

"Why don't we question her here at the inn? She might not be so nervous."

"Good idea."

"And Jane Witherspoon, her helper. I think you've seen her."

"Right. Seen and forgotten."

The waitress brought his food. Charleston, after a sip of coffee, said, "Then later today we get down to the nitty-gritty?"

Before Perkins could answer, Mrs. Charleston spoke up. "It seems like forever, but I know how it is. I've learned by experience." She shook her head in a pretense of dolefulness, and there was love in the eyes she turned on her husband.

Perkins stayed his fork to say, "No end until the end. But it's been a very few days, Mrs. Charleston."

She sighed and said, "I know," then brightened to add, "Chick's enjoying himself."

Charleston grinned and said, "Just like home."

When they were done, Geeta rose and said, "While you two go about your business, I'll go chat with my favorite wine seller."

Perkins got up almost at the same time. "You'll excuse me then. I'll see about arrangements, Chick. It's been a pleasure to meet you, Mrs. Charleston."

Jane Witherspoon was at the counter, registering four arrivals. Mrs. Vaughn was on the phone. Perkins stood and waited.

Finally the Witherspoon woman rang for the bellman, looked to Perkins and asked, "May I help you, Inspector?" He didn't know whether she was Mrs. or Miss.

"Yes, if I could talk to both of you."

"Both of us? Together?"

"I'm sorry. Both of you, but one at a time."

Mrs. Vaughn, through with the phone, stood up and stepped to the counter.

He said, "We have a few questions to ask. We thought you might prefer to meet us here, rather than in the incidents room. Can you suggest a place?"

"Oh, dear," Mrs. Vaughn said, "I just go to pieces over anything like this. I don't know what's the matter with me."

Perkins said gently, "No need to feel that way with us. None at all, Mrs. Vaughn. We're really not monsters, just men fumbling around for the truth."

"Thank you." She breathed deep. "I feel more at ease. I try to keep a room vacant for emergencies. It's close by. Would it do?"

"I'm sure. Are there chairs enough?"

"There will be." She summoned the bellman and told him to take two chairs to Room Ten.

"And now," Perkins said to both, "Will one of you please ring the incidents room and ask Sergeant Goodman to join us here?"

Jane Witherspoon headed for the phone.

"Perhaps you want to go first?" Perkins suggested to Mrs. Vaughn.

Charleston showed up then and, two minutes later, Goodman. Perkins asked Mrs. Vaughn if she'd please lead the way.

There were three straight chairs and a rocker in the room, in addition to a bed, a bedside table, a chest of drawers and a pants presser. A door gave onto a closet and a bath. Standard equipment, Perkins thought, as he asked Mrs. Vaughn to take the rocker. He and Charleston took straight chairs facing her. Goodman removed his chair a bit so as not to be prominent as he took notes.

Perkins nodded to Charleston. "You have questions, Chick?" Charleston was just as good an interrogator as he himself, maybe better. Let him have the floor.

Charleston said, "Mrs. Vaughn, we're sorry to have to disturb you. We can imagine how you feel. But there's one thing we'd like to make sure of."

She murmured, "I'll help if I can."

"It's the question of locking up on Monday night before the murder. Can you tell us for sure, were the side and back doors locked?"

She answered, "Oh, dear. It seems so long ago. You know, the nights and days just run together. It's arrivals and departures, new guests coming in and guests going out, new faces, known faces and hellos and goodbyes. When was that night again?"

"Monday night, April 21. The body was found the following morning."

"One of us always locks up, Larry or myself."

"And did you that night?"

"We must have. It's — you know — a habit."

"And that's as sure as you can be?"

She put a hand to her head and closed her eyes as if to see inside her skull. "I'm so vague."

"I'm sure you can see the importance of the question. With no signs of a break-in, with the doors all locked, then . . . "

"Then it must have been one of us, someone already inside."

"Yes. Now Larry Bates says he seems to remember that you trailed along with him, just to be sociable, as he locked the doors?"

"Sometimes I do. He comes from nothing and needs encouragement. Sometimes I do."

"That's as much as you can say?"

"I'm afraid so."

Perkins coughed and said, "Excuse me."

Charleston crossed his legs, waited a second, and went on, "Let's leave that question then. Maybe later you'll remember and tell us. Now, Mrs. Vaughn, what was your opinion of the late Mr. Smith. Did you like him? Dislike him? What did you observe?"

"I think I've answered that question before. He was a guest, that was all."

"And nobody said anything to you? Nobody expressed an opinion?"

"Nobody, Mr. Charleston. No one at all."

Perkins reflected that she was probably telling the truth. In consideration of her health, no one chose to bother her.

"And you heard nothing that night, nothing out of the way?"

"Nothing. I've answered that before, too."

"What do you know about the trouble in the bar, the fight that preceded Mr. Smith's death?"

"Only what was reported to me. It seems Mr. Tarvin tried to hit Mr. Smith and missed, being drunk, and then Constable Doggett came in, and they put Mr. Tarvin in jail."

"And that's all you made of it?"

"No, sir. I told Mr. Tarvin never to come back."

"How?"

"By mail to his company in Bath."

Charleston said, "Thank you, Mrs. Vaughn. I think that's all, unless Inspector Perkins has more questions." Perkins shook his head. "Would you ask Jane Witherspoon to come in?"

As she rose to leave, Perkins said, "Now that wasn't so bad, was it?" and received a quick smile in return. He added before she could go out the door, "Is this Witherspoon person single or what?"

"A Mrs. She's a widow."

Jane Witherspoon entered confidently and seated herself in the rocker without being asked. She wore a green blouse that gave color to her face and life to hair that showed a little gray. She was, Perkins thought, not too old to bear looking at twice, or more.

"Mrs. Witherspoon," Charleston began, "we go through a lot of routine in any murder case, unless, of course, it's open and shut."

"You can forget the preliminaries, Mr. Charleston," she broke in. "Ask your questions, and I'll tell you what I know."

"Fair enough, but I hope you'll go beyond what you actually know. You may have suspicions. You may have noticed something that would arouse ours. So don't feel hesitant in your answers. You'll find us discreet."

She laughed lightly. "That's the adulterer's word. Discreet."

"Could be. But it's murder, not adultery, that concerns us."

"That sounds kind of stuffy. I bet you think so, too."

"No bet."

"A little fun never hurt an investigation, did it?"

"Just laugh in the face of murder?" Charleston grinned as he spoke. Perkins imagined Chick was enjoying the exchange. For that matter, he was himself.

"I've learned to laugh at many things," she replied, sobering. "Had to, you know."

Charleston nodded. "Yes, I know. We all do. Now what about the murder of Mr. Smith? What can you tell us?"

"I hear a knife was stuck in him. Rose said she found him dead. That's the sum of my knowledge. Just hearsay, I suppose."

"What about surmises?"

"That's too strong a word. I haven't any." A slender hand waved the suggestion away.

"Let's approach the matter in another way, if you will."

"If I will, Mr. Charleston? You mean *you* will."

"Forgive the loose language." A grin came and went on his face. "Was there anything about Mr. Smith that struck you particularly? Anything in his manner? His expression? Anything?"

"He liked women."

"So do most men, including myself."

Her hand fanned at him in disgust. "You know what I mean without my spelling it out. He was woman-crazy."

"Some woman in particular?"

"All women in general so far as I could observe. Any woman would know. Around us he put on such a winning manner while his eyes seemed to see under our clothes."

"A lecher, was he? Any success?"

Her laugh pealed out. "How would I know? I can speak just for myself."

"And?"

"You're just too nosy, Mr. Charleston." She was still laughing. "If I had succumbed to his charms, I would deny it, wouldn't I? So what's the purpose in denial when I'm innocent? He tried me, and I chilled him. That's the fact."

"What about the other women in their party of five? No, just the one other woman, since Mrs. Post is his sister."

"Mrs. Witt?"

"Yes."

"Again, how would I know? But I got the impression that she merely endured him, and that by the hardest."

Perkins sighed silently. For no sensible reason the suggestion of a union there had disturbed him.

Charleston went on, "What about the men? How did they behave toward him?"

"Mr. Witt seemed friendly enough. But Mr. Post, that was different."

"How so?"

She was silent for a moment, then took a breath and answered, "It's my notion that Mr. Post couldn't stand him. They never spoke to each other. They were like enemies. You could feel the heat just being around them."

Charleston rubbed his jaw, nodded his head, and said, "Did you notice any strangers in or around the inn on the night of the murder? Anyone to suspect? And did you hear any strange noises that night?"

"No to the idea of strangers, Mr. Charleston. And I sleep in a cottage on the grounds, so I wouldn't have heard anything."

"You work here, but you're more than paid help. Is it fair to say that?"

"I suppose. We're lifelong friends, you know. And since that heart attack Mrs. Vaughn hasn't been up to much. She's so nervous, for one thing, afraid of everything, anything official especially."

"Is it because she might get in trouble as an innkeeper, because Peter Tarvin got drunk in her bar?"

"I doubt that. Who's going to complain? You?"

"Not likely."

"I just hope she can keep on with the inn."

"Who has keys to the inn?"

"I don't. I think only Mrs. Vaughn and the night porter. That's to the best of my knowledge. You're asking yourself how anyone got inside, if anyone did."

"Right."

"But there are no close trees with handy branches, no convenient downspouts."

"And no signs of a break-in," he said.

"Wizard at work." She smiled at him.

Charleston rose and extended his hand. "I believe that ends the inquisition, Mrs. Witherspoon, but let's play word games again sometime."

"And remember how useful is that word 'discreet.' "

Perkins held up a hand. "We've got no statement from you in the files, Mrs. Witherspoon. Sergeant Goodman will type out this conversation, show it to you, and ask you to sign it if it's not in error."

"I'll bend my mind to it," she answered and went out.

At the desk Perkins thanked Mrs. Vaughn for the use of the room and asked if the Posts and Witts were in.

She said they were. Perkins consulted his watch and said to Charleston, "'We have time for one more before lunch. Take your pick."

"Mrs. Post then, if you agree."

"I'll phone her. Ask her to come over. How about waiting for her, Sergeant?"

"Sure thing."

The sky was clear, though a trifle misty. The incidents room smelled stale. Perkins had no sooner opened the windows than Mrs. Post and Goodman came in.

"It's kind of you to appear again," Perkins told her. "Won't you have a seat? Mr. Charleston has agreed to do the talking today."

Mrs. Post was dressed in dark clothes again, a suit too heavy for the weather. She wore a small, black beret and little earrings set with red stones. Her shoes appeared new but workaday.

"I know you think we're being a nuisance, Mrs. Post," Charleston began, "but we are determined to find out who murdered your brother. I'm sure you want us to do that."

She gave a bare nod, her face impassive. The dead, inexpressive face of a statue, Perkins thought. Didn't anything ever get to her?

"After all, it was your brother who was killed," Charleston reminded her. "Surely you want to see justice done?"

She sat mute, her eyes on him.

"Is there a reason behind your silence?"

He persisted when she didn't answer. "Your husband hated him. Is that why you don't answer, for fear your husband killed him? Speak up, Mrs. Post. Are you shielding Mr. Post? What are we to believe?"

This was really bearing down, Perkins thought. This verged on the brutal. He had started to shake his head when Mrs. Post bent forward, shoulders hunched. A small despairing sound came from her. It was impossible, this big hulk of a woman, this piece of statuary, to be folded and weeping. Even as he thought so, a great sob shook her, and sobbing words came out. "It's so hard, so hard. No one can know."

Charleston sat quiet, letting her cry, but on his good face was a look of misery. He took a handkerchief from his pocket and pressed it in her hands.

She began speaking again, the words choking out, spaced by short breaths. "He was good to me. Always good. His little sister. He called me that . . . even when I grew up. His little sister."

No one spoke. It seemed no one breathed except Mrs. Post. She raised her head then, the handkerchief against a cheek, and said, "I'm sorry."

"No, Mrs. Post." Charleston might have been speaking to a child. "No need to be sorry. You'll feel better by telling."

She lowered her head again. "Ben came, and I loved him, and we got married. He's a good husband." She put the handkerchief to her eyes again and tried not to cry. "Such a good husband, and it's been so hard, and I've tried and tried. God knows I've tried."

Charleston's voice was still soothing. "We're sure of that. Rest easy there."

"And we moved to America. Ollie joined us about three years later, and Ollie and Ben went into business, sometimes together, sometimes with Walter Witt, sometimes alone. He did well, off and on, Ben did."

Perkins loaded his pipe but didn't light it. Maybe it had been wrong to load it. Any distraction might end the spell in the room.

He needn't have worried, for Mrs. Post went on, raising her head, then bending it again. "Then Ben concluded that Ollie had done him wrong in some deal or other, and he set out to whip him." Her head moved back and forth. "I was there. I tried to stop it, but Ben kept hitting Ollie, and then Ollie . . . he was terribly strong — put his arm around Ben and brought one of Ben's arms up behind his back and, holding him and bringing the arm up more, made Ben say he'd had enough. Then Ollie let go his hold and slapped Ben's face, slapped it again and then again while tears streamed down Ben's face."

Abruptly she fell silent and seemed to wilt until Charleston asked, "Would you like some water, Mrs. Post?"

She didn't answer but bowed her head again while fresh sobs shook her. "There's no one alive left to grieve. No one but me."

Goodman came forward with a glass of water and put it in her hand, then stepped back to his chair.

"No one, Mrs. Post? No one at all?" Charleston asked. "No family?"

"No one."

"Aren't there other Smiths around here?"

"Plenty, I suppose, but no kin of ours."

"Your parents are both dead?"

"A long time ago."

"No aunts, uncles, cousins living?"

"None living. We had an aunt. She married a German and went to live there. We lost track of her. I think she's dead."

"Go on, Mrs. Post."

"There was an uncle, too. He was a sailor and lost at sea in 1917. A bomb or something. No children."

"I see. Thanks. Now about your brother. Didn't he ever marry?"

Tears still shimmered in her eyes. "Yes. After Ben and I went to America. It didn't work out."

"Did you know his wife?"

"I never met her. I don't know her maiden name and not even when they were married. I don't know for sure that they were, but I guess so."

"Didn't your brother ever speak of her?"

"He was bitter, so bitter. I could tell that. He kept it to himself."

"Any children?"

"I think one child, from something he let drop, but I never could get anything more out of him."

"We're grateful to you, Mrs. Post. We'll have to consider what you've told us, see whether it helps us."

"That's what I was afraid of. That's why I didn't want to tell you. You think Ben killed him. You think my husband killed my brother. But I swear to you that isn't so." Her voice rose. The words came faster. "It can't be true. It doesn't fit."

"Why not, Mrs. Post?"

"Because that kind of killing, that stabbing with a knife, wouldn't have satisfied Ben. It wouldn't have eased his humiliation one little bit. To feel right, to feel proud in his head again, he would have had to whip him with his fists. He would have had to make him say 'enough' and slap his face afterwards."

She rose, wiped her eyes once more and tossed the handkerchief on Perkins's desk. She straightened, reassembling her being, and stepped to the door, herself again, a whole woman. Maybe.

Chapter Twelve

CONSTABLE RENDELL, whom Perkins had asked to scout around on the chance of picking up something significant, joined them before they reached the Stag and Hind. Perkins steered him to the side of the walk out of the foot traffic. "Had lunch?" he asked.

"Just a little while ago."

"So. Anything?"

"Two items. Among the strangers, a professional man, so he seemed, here in Upper Beechwood on the afternoon of the murder. He kind of stood out. No sign of him since. Two, a young fellow, a stranger, was around on the same day, too. He bought cigarettes, and the clerk that waited on him said he talked like a Cotswold man but was dressed up pretty fancy, like for a wedding or feast."

"Yes?"

"That's all, except the young bloke seemed interested in girls, them that might listen to reason."

"Good work, Rendell," Perkins said. "Now look in the records and see if you can find anything relating to the marriage of Oliver Smith. The bride's name. She may have been from around here. Children, if any. Dig it out, Constable."

At the pub Perkins absently ordered pork pie and a pint and went with Goodman and Charleston to a table.

Later, back in the incidents room, he reported what Rendell had told him. "Maybe something, maybe not a damn thing."

"Professional man, as distinct from a businessman," Charleston said, stroking his jaw. "Did he make that point?"

"More or less, I'd say."

"Sergeant," Charleston said, "the names of the men who lodged at the inn that night. You understand, murder night. Are they in your file?"

"Yes, sir." Goodman came over, leafed through the reports, and said finally, "Here they are. Thornton, McCarthy, Burroughs — "

"Stop right there." He turned to Perkins. "Clayton, Clayton and Burroughs. That's Post's firm of solicitors in London, Sergeant?"

"Yes, sir."

The inspector said, "I will be damned."

"Isn't it likely that Smith used that firm, too? Why not? No conflict. Stands to reason."

"Right. We'll tackle him." Perkins smiled without much mirth. "We move forward. Perhaps not forward, but we're moving. So now, that young fellow Rendell mentioned, we'll hear more from him on that. Let's go. I want to see Walter Witt." He didn't say that he wanted to see Mrs. Witt, too, to close the afternoon with the sight and sound of her in his senses. Damn foolishness, but there it was.

Goodman rose and went to the door, saying, "I'll see where he is. I notified him earlier."

"That man Burroughs," Perkins said. "No time like the present."

He lifted the phone, dialed, and after a few minutes, was

given the firm's number. A minute after that he said, "Mr. Burroughs, please." Then, "Mr. Burroughs, this is Detective Chief Inspector Fred Perkins at Upper Beechwood. We'd like to talk to you." He quit speaking and listened. "Oh, yes, so you do know. Could we come to your office for a chat? Burford? Tomorrow? About noon? That would be fine. I'll have my sergeant and an American officer with me. He's helping in the investigation. Charles Charleston is his name. Right. The Lamb Inn."

"Well, that's arranged," he said, hanging up the receiver. "Convenient for us. Burroughs has an appointment in Burford. That's better than London." Goodman entered with Witt then. "Good afternoon, Mr. Witt. Have a seat. We have some questions."

Witt was dressed in a lightweight, gray suit, complete with vest. With his gray shirt he wore a blue tie. His wire-framed glasses glinted in a slanting shaft of light. He sat facing Perkins, as alert as a sparrow. Behind his glasses his eyes seemed to be smiling. Perkins looked from him to Charleston to Goodman, who was ready with his notebook. "My colleague here, Mr. Charleston, has the questions. Don't be irritated if you've answered the questions before."

"Repetition leads to conviction, as our late Nazi friend, Dr. Goebbels, was wont to say." He looked around pleasantly. "In other words, say a thing often enough, and it becomes popular belief. Fire away, Mr. Charleston."

"A few things then. You've already given Inspector Perkins your full name and address?"

"Right you are. And accounted for my presence here."

"So you say." Charleston folded his hands and for a long instant studied the man. "What about the others? What about your companions?"

Witt smiled. He wasn't a sparrow. He was a banty rooster. "I assume you will consider the presence of my wife as being in the nature of things."

"Quite." Charleston cast an amused glance at Perkins as he said the word. "And is it, was it, in the nature of things that Mr. Smith should be with you?"

"He had some business here. More than that, he was born in the Cotswolds and hadn't been back since he left England years ago."

"And Mr. and Mrs. Post?"

"As you know, she is, or was, Oliver Smith's sister. Like him, she wanted to see the Cotswolds again."

"Very cozy, Mr. Witt. Very nice indeed. So you all got together, you great friends, and decided to come in a sort of close family group?"

"Now, Mr. Charleston, I see no need for sarcasm. It just turned out to be convenient for us to come together."

"So convenient that I wonder."

"Do you also wonder about people on a tour, how they get together? People from here and there, from near and far, and there they all are on a coach or plane, friendly as next-door neighbors."

"You were hardly that friendly. We are told that Mr. Post hated Mr. Smith, and I suppose vice versa. That must have made for merriment."

"They kept their feelings under good control. I don't ask that my friends be friends with one another."

"Were they personal or merely business friends of yours?"

"I suppose you could say both. Off and on I've been in business with them, together or singly, a good many times."

"Do you have any idea what business Mr. Smith had here?"

"Not really. Something to do with an estate. He didn't confide in me. He was a close-mouthed man."

"We have gathered in our questioning that you, almost alone, were on friendly terms with Mr. Smith."

"Was I?"

"Don't dodge the point, Mr. Witt. Why was he disliked?"

Witt's gaze went from Charleston to Perkins to Goodman.

He wore a small smile. "Why not consult Dr. Freud? He might know. I don't."

"I'm not so sure of that. Now what's beyond my understanding is why Mr. Post, hating Mr. Smith as he did, should consent to travel with Mr. Smith at the mere urging of his wife?"

"Perhaps you don't appreciate her powers of persuasion."

Charleston grunted. "Maybe so," he said. "There are other things I don't appreciate. Your explanations, for instance. I find them leaky."

"I swear that is too bad — when the truth won't hold water. And I'll add just this, for your enlightenment. We have venture capital and are looking for opportunities for investment. And I hope you haven't overlooked the fact that my twin brother lives here, and I wanted to see him again."

"Capital for investment. Where? Here?"

Mr. Witt smiled tolerantly. "Not here. In London perhaps. On the continent maybe, or in South America."

Charleston pointed a finger at him. "You have given reasons for coming here, Mr. Witt. What were your reasons for leaving the United States?"

"Why did the chicken cross the road? To get to the other side, of course. Why did I leave America? To come to England, naturally. I've told you the why of that. Any more questions in that direction, and I stand mute, or should I say 'sit mute'? You are venturing too far afield."

"All right then, to the immediate subject. Did you kill Oliver Smith?"

"From being far afield, you turn to nonsense. Of course I didn't kill him. Didn't want to and didn't do it."

"Do you have any idea who did?"

"None at all. That's your department."

"Your brother says you want him to sell out and throw in with you."

"That's right, and to the best of my knowledge it's not criminal. He hasn't enough opportunity here. I'd like him to realize himself. I want the two of us to live closer than an ocean apart. Is that such a sinful wish, Mr. Charleston?"

"Skip it. Where were you, what did you do on the evening and night of the murder?"

"I reported all that earlier."

"Report it again."

"Beginning when?"

"When you last saw Mr. Smith."

"That would be at dinner Monday night, when I last saw him alive."

"Go on."

"We dined at the inn that evening, the five of us — the Posts, Smith, and my wife and I."

"Did you note anything unusual in your companions?"

"Not really. Smith seemed preoccupied, but then he often was."

"Afterwards?"

"We broke up. The Posts went to their room, and we to ours. Smith said he had some business to attend to."

"What business?"

"The Lord knows."

"He went to the bar later on. Did you know that?"

"Not until the next day, by hearsay. But it was not out of character. He liked a solitary and meditative drink before bedtime. That much I know of him."

"This one seems not to have been very solitary or meditative, either. Did you know he helped subdue a drunk?"

"Not until afterwards, again by hearsay."

Charleston nodded and thought a minute. "So we have you and Mrs. Witt in your room. Early to go to bed, wasn't it?"

"Too early, of course. My wife had a book she wanted to finish, and I involved myself with a chess problem. Do you play chess, Mr. Charleston?"

"Not if I can avoid it. You spent the evening until bedtime that way. Then what?"

"Aren't you invading the privacy of the bedroom, sir?"

"Omit the intimacies, if any. Did you hear anything, anything at all during the time you were there, anything that suggested violence or trouble?"

"Not one thing."

"And yet there was a fight in the bar."

"Our room is some distance away from the bar, and on a different floor. I doubt we would have heard any noises suggesting a fracas even if we hadn't been immersed in our own interests."

"And nothing during the night? You didn't get up and leave the room? You weren't aroused by any sound?"

"No on all counts. It was not until seven o'clock in the morning, my usual time of getting up, that I left what the romantics call dreamland."

Charleston turned from him to Inspector Perkins. "I think that's all, unless Inspector Perkins has more questions."

Perkins answered, "No more."

Witt rose, smiling again. "Good day, gentlemen. Thanks for your enlightenment."

Perkins asked, "Enlightenment?"

"Into the ways of the constabulary." He walked out, confident as ever. Goodman went with him to find Mrs. Witt.

"Satisfied?" Perkins asked of Charleston.

"One slippery customer, and he may know more than he admitted, but I can't see him as a killer."

"No." Perkins opened the door for fresh air, then came back and lighted his pipe, thinking as he did so that the second act canceled the first. No matter. He wanted a smoke.

Mrs. Witt came into the room with Goodman. She looked around the room, her eyes wide and inquiring, and said in a subdued voice that struck Perkins as musical, "Good afternoon. Shall I sit here?"

She had on a blue dress that matched the blue of her eyes. It seemed loose-fitting, yet where it touched her, it clung as if caressing the curves. Her hair appeared to have the shine of the sun in it. A small woman she surely was, small and tidy and good-smelling. A woman well put together. "Yes, do sit down," he said as his eyes ran over her. "Just a few questions we need to ask."

"I'll be happy to answer if I can." She gave a little, uncertain smile, like that of a child in need of assurance.

"Don't be anxious," Perkins hurried to say. "We have to go through routines."

She did appear almost childlike, no matter her perhaps thirty years, childlike and delicate, with the young expression of trust and innocence that nevertheless was a challenge. Perkins tried to think professionally, to ignore the stirring in his breeches.

"It was kind of you to question the others first," she said. He had the feeling she was talking to him alone. "You gave me time to get my thoughts in order." Her dress was drawn up a bit now she was seated, displaying part of a slender leg.

"Mr. Charleston is doing the questioning today," he said. "Your fellow American." He hoped he caught a look of disappointment.

"And fellow Montanan, at least in the broad sense," Charleston said, no doubt to put her at ease. "I'll not ask you your whereabouts on the night of the murder, Mrs. Witt. You answered that question earlier." He smiled, then went on. "None of you have very solid alibis, by the way. The women were with their husbands, and the husbands were with their wives, and where's the real proof either way?"

"I can imagine it would be troublesome."

"Now we're trying to find out all we can about Mr. Smith. Someone had reason to do away with him. What reason? What person? Can you help us at all there?"

"I can't see how. No reason occurs to me." She made a small, helpless gesture. "All I know is I'm not guilty. That's truth. That's gospel, if you wish." Her smile asked assent. Behind it, her teeth were white and even.

"All right," Charleston said. "Now, Mrs. Witt, we know that

some of you and some of the staff didn't like Mr. Smith. At least one of your group hated him. Why, Mrs. Witt?"

Her eyes came to Perkins in appeal. "I don't know that I can explain. Have you asked them?"

"We have, with limited success."

"My husband rather liked him, so that adds up to his being not much of a suspect."

"What were your feelings about him?"

For an instant she seemed uncertain. Her eyes went to Perkins. "I guess nothing much. I was neutral." She straightened her shoulders. "That's it exactly, I was neutral."

"That sounds as if your companions were not."

"Oh, no. I didn't mean that. I just meant I had no particular feelings one way or the other. And I understand my husband. He hasn't time for pettiness. His mind is always full of other things. You could say he's all business. He's a planner. No time to be petty."

"All business. No time for anything but, well, schemes, ways to make money?"

A slender hand came up in protest. "That's harsh, Mr. Charleston, but in the best sense, yes, he's a schemer."

"You weren't at the inquest."

"No, and I don't think that matters. I'm just not morbid."

"You're right. It's not significant. Thanks for talking with us, Mrs. Witt. No more questions today, unless Inspector Perkins wants to ask some."

Perkins said, catching and holding her eyes, "Are you sure you can't help us more, Mrs. Witt?"

"I don't see how."

"Be sure, Mrs. Witt. Be sure. We'd hate to find you knew more than you told us."

"Please," she said. Her eyes were pleading. "There's nothing more to say. Don't accuse me, Inspector."

"Accuse you? I just thought perhaps you'd overlooked something."

She smiled a sort of sad smile. "Yes, Inspector." She rose, stood for a moment, said, "Goodbye, gentlemen," and went out the door.

"You seemed to think she knew more than she admitted," Charleston said to Perkins then.

Perkins knew he squirmed and stopped it. "I just wasn't positive. And you still suspect the three men were involved in some graft, some kind of roguery?"

"A suspicion."

"But nothing really to do with our case?"

"I doubt it. Has headquarters reported anything from the American end?"

"Not yet. Pretty early, I'd say, even if Hawley got right to it. What're you doing tonight?"

"I'm going to have dinner with my wife, if she'll still speak to me."

"Me, I've got to report to headquarters yet."

"So goodnight, Fred. Goodnight, Sergeant."

Sergeant Goodman waved a hand and answered, "Wish I had a wife to go to, even if she wouldn't talk to me."

A wife to go home to, Perkins thought. A woman to have. He moved restlessly. And leisure to enjoy her, with no time pressing him. All these interviews, and what had been the good of them? Questions and answers and no results, and here it was the fourth day. The case might as well be in the hands of that Simple Simon, Doggett. And where was he, by the way? Hawley would rejoice at their failure. He'd be quick to seize on anything that might argue for a change of investigators.

He rose to his feet. "Let's get the bloody hell out of here, Sergeant."

Chapter Thirteen

AFTER CHICK AND PERKINS left her that morning, Geeta set out for Mr. Ebersole's store. She thought she looked good in her tweeds. It was still cool enough for them, though the sky was unclouded.

She felt the moist air on her face. It made her skin feel fresh and young, as if every wrinkle were smoothing out. Unlike Montana, she thought, feeling disloyal, where wind and aridity dried out the skin and made hair hard to manage.

An antique shop she hadn't visited stood just across the street from Ebersole's, and she dropped in there for a minute to inquire about flow-blue. No luck, as she had expected.

At the store she said, "Good morning, Mr. Ebersole." He was arranging fruit in the front, wearing his black suspenders and white shirt. A man was stocking shelves in the rear.

"Well, Mrs. Charleston, it's a pleasure to see you," he answered. "Some more of that good French wine?"

"Yes, Mr. Ebersole, after a while." She gave him her smile. "Do you have time to talk this morning?"

"Plenty of time. I even had time to stand still and look out the windows and watch people passing. I saw you entering the antique shop across the way."

"I was looking for china, flow-blue china. I can't seem to find much of it, and what there is is so expensive." She drew a breath. "But I really came to finish our talk about the Hawthornes." She went on to say, "It surprises me that you know my name."

He smiled his old man's smile. "It shouldn't. In the real tourist season, with crowds in the village, I wouldn't have known. But in the slack season we take note, especially of women good to look at."

She returned his smile and waited.

He backed up to a stand of vegetables and rested against it. It struck her that he was tired and maybe not well. "But perhaps you'd rather tell me another time?"

"Oh, no, no. I'm all right. You said you were interested in your ancestry, and I told you about the Hawthornes, the old Hawthornes. You could go to Scotland to inquire."

"I wish I could, but I can't. We're here on vacation, my husband and I, and the time is nearly up."

"I see. Then there's old Mr. Steele here in the village. He knew them and might be able to tell you more."

"I've seen him."

Mr. Ebersole shook his head.

"But you mentioned a Hawthorne woman from a later time."

"Oh, yes."

"Can you tell me more? Were they related?"

"That I wouldn't know. I doubt it. She lived here just a few years and kept pretty much to herself."

A customer came in, and the man in the rear came forward to wait on him. Mr. Ebersole looked on with little apparent interest. He shifted against the vegetable display and breathed out a sighing breath.

Should she question him further? Geeta asked herself. He looked tired to death, but he waited for her to speak.

"You knew her?" she dared to ask.

"Not to say knew," he answered. "She used to come into the

shop, buy what she wanted, and take her leave, with no time to visit or even say hello. She rented a little flat somewhere in the village. Not much money, I gathered, and no close friends I knew of."

She felt pushy, asking more questions, but perhaps she had only one or two more. "Didn't she ever marry?"

"Yes. Married one of the Smiths from around here."

"Were there children?"

"One. A baby boy, as I recall."

"What happened to them?"

"The whole family disappeared. Dropped from sight. No one seemed to know where, and no one seemed to care."

"And that was the last of them?"

"We thought so for a long time, that is if we thought about them at all. You know, time goes by and memories are short, and very few in the village would have remembered them. They might have had some dim recollection if reminded."

Mr. Ebersole sighed and waited for breath. "About four years ago she returned to the Cotswolds, to Lower Beechwood or just outside it, to a big farm. Quite a holding it was, owned by her sister, a Mrs. Huntley."

He was awfully pale now, and Geeta wished he would not try to go on.

"The sister was a widow, and she was rich. She owned the estate and had other possessions, and they lived, so I've heard, like wealthy people. Going to London to shop and all that." He shook his head as if in slow wonder at the doings of the rich. "It's my idea that Mrs. Huntley supported her sister all along, at least as far as her husband would permit. Then, when her husband died, she invited the sister to live with her."

"Happy ending," Geeta said, hoping Mr. Ebersole was through.

He caught his breath and continued, almost in a whisper, "Not so happy. Here, about two years ago, Mrs. Huntley died, leaving everything to her sister. Then, almost exactly a year later, Mrs. Smith herself died. The son, Tom Smith, inherited. He's about twenty-two years old."

"Thank you, Mr. Ebersole, that's enough. All I wanted to know. Don't you think you'd better rest?"

He made a little wave with one hand. "Not all," he said. "Just the other day, maybe last week it was, word of trouble got around. Trouble over the property. Someone was laying claim to part of it. Or that was the report."

With the last words Mr. Ebersole's body started to slant. She caught him before he could fall. She called out, "Please help."

The assistant, done with the customer, hurried to them. "Office in back. Couch there," he told her. Together they took Mr. Ebersole to the office and laid him down. "I'm all right," he was whispering. "All right."

"Brandy?" Geeta asked the helper. "Spirits somewhere?"

The man went to a desk, opened it, and said "Scotch?"

"My husband would prescribe it."

He poured a measure and brought it over and held it to Mr. Ebersole's lips, but the old man shook his head, took the glass in his hand, and swallowed the whisky in a gulp. After a minute he let out a satisfied "Ah."

From the front of the store someone called. Mr. Ebersole's assistant said, "I'll be right back," and left the office.

"Don't need him now," Mr. Ebersole said, turning his head toward Geeta. He managed a smile. "Thanks for catching me. Don't like to bounce."

"Do you want more whisky?"

"One's enough." His hand went to his throat. "Did you unbutton my collar?"

"It seemed best."

"Woman's touch."

"You don't need to talk, Mr. Ebersole. Just rest."

The assistant looked in the door, nodded and disappeared.

"Nothing to worry about. Just a little spell. I get them sometimes. Age, you know."

"You shouldn't be working."

"Now, now, my dear. No work and I'm dead. How are you spending the time?"

"I find things to do."

"While your man's sleuthing, eh? What do you find?"

"I'm interested in old things, not just old, but things I like. Antiques."

"Seen anything?" Mr. Ebersole sat up slowly.

"Lots of things. Furniture too heavy to take with us and too expensive besides. But my great disappointment is that flow-blue. I could take a few smaller pieces with us without trouble. But all I really found was one beautiful big platter, too big and too expensive. One shop told me American dealers were buying it all up."

"Flow-blue," he said, his eyes distant. "In my day it was just blue and white china. I remember. I remember." He put his thumbs under his suspenders, his fingers on his thin stomach, and was silent.

She said, "I'll keep looking. Maybe I'll get lucky. I love the way the cobalt blue penetrates, like a blue shadow on the other side. I have a few pieces."

She fell silent, too, thinking about it.

Into the silence he said, not in self-pity, "I'm an old man." She waited. "Old, but I believe I have my wits about me."

"I'll speak for your wits."

As he spoke, he seemed to be questioning himself. "But is it age, is it the mark of age, to act on impulse, to decide without thinking?" His eyes, clouded by questions, lifted to her and asked for an answer.

Too many subjects, she thought. Too many concerns. Smith and Smith again. One Smith dead, the other alive. Smiths and flow-blue, and flow-blue and Smiths. And here was an old man, a gentle old man, wondering about his age and his mind.

"How can I answer, Mr. Ebersole? I don't know enough. It would depend, I suppose. Myself, I'm inclined to act on hunches. Sometimes they're wrong, though."

He said, "They belong in America." What did he mean, she asked herself? Was she wrong about his wits?

He began slowly then, his eyes far away, with the years deep in his face. "We were going to America once, my bride and I. We were young, our blooming time, you know, and we saw it as a light, the light of the world, I guess you could say. Or it was the promise waiting there?" His mouth closed. His eyes might be seeing that promise again. "We planned. Oh, we planned. We had faith. We believed. We'd take ship as soon as we had money enough. We'd sail to the bright shores."

"Yes, yes," she said with hardly half her mind on his words.

He interrupted his story to repeat, "Money enough. Yes," he said then, "we made ready as far as our purse allowed. We bought some furniture and linens and silverware, all to go on board with us, and we ordered place settings for eight. We would be sociable in our new home."

Gazing at the worn face, gentle with its memories, Geeta thought he might be in America now in his mind, or on the verge of sailing with his hard-earned housewares and furnishings and his bride and their hopes.

His voice went on, "It was out of production by then, but we found a London store that had it, blue and white, eight settings, Touraine pattern, made by Henry Alcock."

He paused, took a couple of shallow breaths and continued with haltings as if finding the words hard to say. "We were almost ready. Then, before the china arrived, my bride took sick and died. A short illness, meningitis, they thought it was. Yes, and the flow-blue came too late. It's in my little house now. I never unpacked the boxes. I couldn't bring myself to. Couldn't bring myself to send them back, either. Crazy, I guess."

"No, Mr. Ebersole, not crazy." Geeta brought her handkerchief to her eyes. "I'm so sorry."

He sat, still as a carving, his face bleak with old suffering. He was, she thought, too old for tears. He'd shed them all long ago.

He spoke softly. "It belongs in America. That's where it should be. That's where my bride would want it."

She wished he'd stop before he undid her.

"In America, in the hands of someone who loves it, not to be auctioned off when I die, not to go to nephews I never see. Yes, America. It's yours, Mrs. Charleston."

She cried out, "No, no, Mr. Ebersole. You're not thinking right. I can't."

"Not even to oblige an old man?"

She burst out crying.

It didn't bear thinking about — old Mr. Ebersole, his dead bride, the flow-blue and the gift of it. One couldn't rejoice over a gift given from heartache. It and its history lay too heavy on the spirit. She protested. She tried to refuse, but could not bring herself to an outright rejection, he was so insistent and looked so frail and fluttery. Time would ease her feelings, for that was a habit of time. She patted his arm, said goodbye and went out of the store, forgetting the bottle of wine.

Outside she stood still, oblivious of people, while her mind churned. Flow-blue and the name Smith, and hadn't Mrs. Witt said something about Oliver Smith and business in connection with an estate? A long jump to a conclusion, but still. . . . And the Hawthorne woman and the relationship, if any, the reason she had come to see Mr. Ebersole in the first place! Driven from her mind, almost.

She'd feel better when she saw Chick, but he would be busy with Perkins or Goodman or both. Better not to interrupt them. Better not to be seen as the hysterical woman, even if Chick would never think so. What she knew could wait, couldn't it?

So be practical, she told herself as she stood there. Get on with research. Chick wouldn't mind, but did she dare drive the rented car on English roads? Eight miles to Lower Beechwood, they said. Eight miles and remember to drive on the left.

That was it, then. The keys to the car would be in the room where Chick had left them.

She set out, striding purposefully, dodging the morning shoppers. The inn was quiet, the keys where she thought they'd be. Here was the car at the side of the inn. She unlocked it, entered, and swore at herself when her hand trembled with the key to the ignition in it. Backing up was no problem, and here she was, out on the street where a sign pointed the way to Lower Beechwood. Keep to the left, woman!

She drove slowly, recalling what Chick had said about the right and left hemispheres of the brain. It wasn't difficult if one took it easy. Let the cars in a hurry whiz by. Hello, goodbye, and good luck, you speed demons.

It struck her of a sudden that she was hungry. She didn't wear a watch, but it must be nearly time for lunch, and noon was no time to go calling. On the main street in Lower Beechwood she found a parking place near a pub that called itself the King and Scepter.

Was it all right for a woman to enter a pub unescorted? Was it the proper thing to do? Proper or not, she was hungry. Let the proprieties go hang.

It seemed clean and rather cozy inside. She ordered a ham and cheese sandwich and coffee and took them to a vacant table. A clock on the wall registered eleven-thirty, a half-hour before the noon rush. Two customers sat at one table, and a uniformed policeman at another. She nibbled at her meal, waiting until the policeman finished his beer and rose to his feet. Then she called, "Officer."

He came to her table, nodding, and greeted her with a "Yes ma'am."

"I wonder, can you tell me the way to the home of Mr. Tom Smith?"

"Young Mr. Smith, you mean? Him with the pounds?"

"I wouldn't know. He owns an estate of some kind, I believe."

"That's your man, if you want to see him."

"Why wouldn't I?"

"Oh, nothing. Tastes differ is all. To get there, drive ahead to the next street and turn left. About a mile and a half out on the right, there's his place. A big stone house, it is, with stone pillars at the entrance to the drive. You can call it an estate all right."

"Thank you, Officer."

He smile down at her. "No harm done, ma'am."

She dawdled over her sandwich and, when her coffee was finished, went for another cup. The first noontime customers drifted in. When the place began filling, she rose and went out to her car and sat there waiting for the slow minutes to pass.

When it seemed near enough time for a visit, she started the engine and drove on, going slowly so as not to arrive when Smith was lunching.

The day was fine, warmer now, the sky deeper, no breeze even whispering. It came to her mind that Montana was raw, with the sun and the wind almost constants, and the grass tan for want of rain. Here everything was as green as the Emerald City when Dorothy landed in Oz. She missed Montana.

She found the stone pillars and turned in. The house rose, tawny, at the end of a curving drive. Beyond the house, to the left, a few sheep were grazing, and farther on she saw what she thought might be deer. In England deer must be raised for the market, for venison was often listed on menus. Roe deer, Chick said they were. A Bentley stood gleaming in front of the house. It would make her rented car look like the last of a scrap yard.

A young man was playing with a pup on the front lawn. He quit playing and looked at her, the ball in his hand, as Geeta braked to a stop.

She called out, "Good day, Mr. Smith."

He didn't answer. He just stood there while the dog jumped for the ball. Geeta got out of the car and walked toward him. Then he said, "Don't bother me. Go away. I'm not buying anything."

His face had the look of pout. His lower lip thrust out, like the spout on a pitcher.

"I'm not selling anything, Mr. Smith. My maiden name was Hawthorne."

He took that news without expression.

"That must mean something to you."

He spoke then. "Yeah. Maybe poor relatives."

"I'm not poor, and I'm beginning to hope you're no relative of mine. I'd hate a blot on the family."

She turned back toward the car, so hot with anger it was hard to breathe.

"Hawthorne," he called to her. She walked on. "That was my mother's name."

"I know that."

"Well, well, what else?"

It seemed silly, talking over her shoulder, so she turned around. "She married a man by the common name of Smith. I'd call that quite a comedown." It felt good to needle this uncivil sprout, even at the cost of snobbery.

He answered, "It was." She hadn't stung him after all. "The son of a bitch."

She made as if to leave again until he said, "Well, put your questions. I'll take the time."

Yes, she thought, busy as he was, with so much work demanding his young attention, he'd take the time. Gracious of him.

The pup was whining for the ball.

"Not such an important question," she said, damping her dislike, "but isn't that pup a Highland terrier?"

"That's him. Fine line. Cost me two hundred pounds."

"Is your ancestry Scottish?"

"Not that I know of. Why?"

"It seems my Hawthorne ancestors were. I'm trying to trace my family, and I thought your mother, having the same name, might have told you something to help me. She might even have been a distant relative."

He was shaking his head. "My mother came from the Midlands, from around Manchester."

"She must have told you something about the Hawthornes, her father's family."

"You're wrong there. She never hardly mentioned them." He nodded his head as if agreeing with himself. "I guess it was because they died early. I don't remember them. It was her mother's side of the family she talked about."

"I see. I'm afraid I've bothered you for nothing."

He threw the ball, and the pup chased after it.

He ignored her apology. "No wonder she hardly ever talked about the Hawthornes. All she ever got from that side of the family was her maiden name." He laughed a short laugh. "And then she traded it for Smith."

"I shouldn't have bothered you, it seems."

Again he ignored her words. "It was my mother's sister, my aunt, that is — it was her that helped us through our bad times, and when she died, she left this place to us." His hand swept out in a proud claim of ownership.

"It's a beautiful place."

"And it's all ours. All mine now, and no one else gets one bit of it. No one."

"That sounds as if somebody had tried?"

He smiled what seemed a victorious smile. "It does now, doesn't it? But it's all over now. No more trouble."

The pup had returned the ball and Smith threw it again and started toward the house. Somewhere a sheep blatted. "Sorry," he said, not looking back. "Got things to do."

She told him, "Thanks," not caring if he were out of earshot. It was time to go home, home to the inn. Driving, she caught herself muttering again, "Smith and Smith. Oliver Smith and Tom Smith, and did the twain ever meet?" But there were a lot of Smiths in the world, some of them in the Cotswolds. She dared drive a bit faster. She had so many things to tell Chick.

Chapter Fourteen

AFTER DINNER THAT NIGHT, Perkins walked to Doggett's house. Goodman had stopped off at the incidents room on the way, saying he had typing to do. The place smelled a little musty, and he aired it out. He smoothed the bed he had made too hastily that morning. He emptied an ashtray and washed it. A man couldn't feel right in an untidy place.

But he knew while he attended to these chores that he was trying to shut off thought by doing them. He sat down, got out his pipe, and put it back. Time was a cloud over him. No, it was rushing at him, head on, and it had an ugly face. Hawley coming tomorrow, sniping at him for lack of progress, hinting at putting another man on the case, and maybe contriving to do so, barring a break. He'd managed that trick once before. A vindictive man, Hawley, still sore because Perkins once had expressed quiet doubts about his abilities. Let him be sore then, the bastard. Charleston had Hawley's number all right, but how much longer would he be around? A week would stretch his time, he had said. Perkins would miss him. He was like a good right arm. More than that.

He jumped to his feet and paced the room. It was really a small flat, this room, a combination of sitting room and kitchen, a bedroom and bath. It was neat and adequate and, as Doggett had said, sound-proofed. No ringing telephone in Doggett's flat sounded here.

He stepped into the alcove that was the kitchen, opened a bottle of good Scotch, poured a sizable drink, and took it down in two gulps. He sat in the one big chair, picked a book from an end table, and pitched it back without reading the title. He rose and paced again.

It wasn't enough that time should press him and Hawley be snotty. He had women on the brain. One woman now, one small woman with that look of fresh innocence that was almost a dare. Women. They were the slave-owners, in them the weapon of giving or withholding. And he was a damned slave, ready to forgive all, to slaver in forgiveness, if the withholding woman would give him release. Women and murder. Murder and women. A man lived one hell of a life. And, like a child, felt damned sorry for himself, the numb-skull.

A knock on the door interrupted him. He went to it and flung it open and saw Mrs. Witt and heard her say, "I promised to tell you something."

His voice came out harsh. "It better be good."

"Don't you want to see me?"

"Yes, I want to see you. Come in." He took her jacket and hung it on a rack. It was wet. "Raining?"

"Raining."

"Do you want to sit down?" He motioned toward the big chair and carried a straight-backed one from the alcove.

Before seating himself, he asked, "Do you want a drink?"

"That would be nice. A small one."

He poured two drinks, added a little water, and brought them back. "Cheers," she said, lifting hers.

"Cheers."

"You don't seem very sociable."

"I'm waiting."

"Can't it wait?"

No, it couldn't wait. Not what he was thinking about. He rose from his chair, took a couple of steps, bent over and kissed her, spilling a few drops of his drink.

As he drew back to see her reaction, she smiled and said, "Thank you."

He said, with a gesture of his head, "Could we? The bedroom?"

She laughed lightly. "You're a sudden man, Inspector." But she got up, moved into the bedroom, sat on the bed and began taking off her clothes — shoes first, stockings from little feet, her blouse, her skirt. . . . He looked away. It was too much. He'd jump her if he saw more.

She stood up, and he did steal a glance at her, seeing a rather small woman, high-breasted and slender. He heard her say, "Aren't you coming?" She pulled down the spread and settled herself.

"Sure, I'm coming," he answered. He began yanking at his clothes. "I was just enjoying the view." He got up and moved toward her, his hand shielding his erection.

"Why not let it show?" she asked. "It's a statement, isn't it?"

He entered her with a lunge that made her gasp, and then it seemed to him she knew more than any woman before her, knew how to please him in ways beyond his experience.

He came almost immediately, and he could imagine he was pumping all of himself, muscles, sinews, and organs into this clever and welcoming conduit. Return to the womb. Why not? Why not?

Lying at her side afterward, he thought of words like delight, like rapture, like bliss. The wife of years ago had been acquiescent, no more than that. The occasional women had been compliant. He wouldn't think about them. He'd think about what he had, what he would have again.

He said, "You're lovely," and they lay quiet.

The rain came then, a steady patter-patter on the roof. What could be better than this—the heard rain, the room cozy and the woman warm at his side?

He rolled from the bed and went to the bathroom and sponged and dried himself. When he returned, she patted his groin lightly.

"I'm wondering about your husband," he said then.

"Don't worry about him."

"But . . ."

"He's either asleep or studying a chess problem."

"That's crazy."

"You'll understand when I tell you he's impotent. Because he is, he lets me have my occasional freedom. He's a civilized man."

"Poor devil. Missing out on this."

"Thanks."

"I'm not pushing you, but you've almost made me forget the important things you were going to tell me."

"I've kept them in mind."

"Good."

"Oliver Smith was a womanizer."

"We already know that."

"You don't know the extent. He couldn't get enough. Never. Not ever."

"You really believe so?"

"I know so. Throughout our trip he's embarrassed us, making up or trying to make up to every female."

"Including you?"

"Of course. But he's not my type at all. I told him so. Told him to get lost and forget it. He wore a beard then, so big and bushy monkeys could have swung in it."

"Bushy passion," Perkins said, laughing lightly.

"Ben Post wore one, too."

"I suspected so. That's hardly the important thing you're going to tell me, is it?"

"Of course not. I haven't told you that." She waited for him to ask what it was and then went on, "Oliver was sleeping with the maid, Rose Whaley."

"For a fact?"

"I would swear to it. Twice I saw her in the hall and both times she entered his room."

"Natural. To tidy up."

"How long would one room take? Ten or twelve minutes at most. I timed her. Once she stayed twenty minutes, another nearly a half-hour."

"Alone?"

"That's it. Not alone. Oliver was with her. I heard both their voices."

"You've helped me, maybe. But Rose a suspect? Hardly."

"I'm not in the business of suspecting. That's your field. But that Smith. What a beast! He put me in mind of that made-up combination, part goat and part man."

"A satyr."

"And the affliction?"

"Satyriasis, I believe."

"My goodness," she said as he pressed against her. "I do believe you must be afflicted yourself. Good for you. I guess I'm part nymph myself."

They made love again, slower this time and better than ever.

"Now I must go," she said. She began putting her clothes back on. "You don't have to get dressed, not unless you want to. There," she went on, buttoning her blouse. "Thank you for a lovely time, Inspector."

"My name's Fred."

"Mine's Drusilla, Dru for short. So goodnight and thanks, Fred."

"Wait. It's late. I'll see you to the inn."

"Oh, no, not together at this hour. I'll sneak back."

She took her jacket from the rack, opened the door, and said, "It's quit raining."

"Thanks, Drusilla. More than thanks, Dru."

When she had gone, he pulled on a robe, poured another drink and lighted his pipe. He'd offended the rules, being intimate with one who might still be a suspect. Not a suspect to him, though. A sweetheart of a woman, and to hell with the rules. He felt the drink in him. Tomorrow might break the case. He felt better.

Chapter Fifteen

PERKINS WAS FIRST in the incidents room the next morning, his mind dwelling on last night and Drusilla Witt, and he felt quite cheerful, putting them in the back of his head. Today could be a lucky day.

Goodman came in and then Rendell and Charleston. They sat down after exchanging good mornings.

"I'd like to have more inquiring around," Perkins said. "Rendell put us on to Mr. Burroughs, the solicitor, and I'm hoping there's more of that kind of information if we look for it. Rendell, I'd like for you to go back to that tobacco store clerk and see if you can't dig up something more."

"Yes, sir."

"Now where's Constable Doggett? He's the man for this kind of thing. Knows everybody. Where is he?"

Goodman answered, "Last I knew, he was looking into the business of some stolen sheep."

"I want him."

Goodman got up, said, "Yes, sir," and went out the door.

"Something on your mind, Chick?"

"Sure is. Thank my wife. A young fellow named Tom

Smith inherited quite a spread and a good deal of money. That's in Lower Beechwood."

"Smith?"

"Yep. Smith. He's a punk. Purse-proud and pushy."

"Smith and Smith. But there's one hell of a lot of Smiths around."

"Right. There's more, though. From something he let fall, Geeta got the impression there was a quarrel over the estate."

"That makes it tighter."

"Sure, when we know what Oliver Smith was here for. Business in connection with an estate, they said."

Perkins began filling his pipe. "We have to see that man Burroughs!"

"That's right, noon today."

The door swung open. Goodman took one step inside. "Doggett's dead!"

"Dead?" Perkins was out of his chair. "Dead! What in hell?"

"Somebody beat his skull in."

Perkins clamped a hand to his head. "That's all we need. Where, Goodman?"

"At his home."

"Murder weapon?"

"A spurtle."

"What in Christ's name is that?"

"Scottish utensil. Wood. For cracking shellfish. Like a small bat. The murderer broke it, hitting Doggett."

"I can't believe it."

"I made sure he was dead, sir."

"Broken into? The house?"

"No. Door was unlocked. I left it that way."

Perkins shook himself straight. "Let's go." He led the way out.

The day was overcast, gloomy with death, Perkins thought. Right in the house where he had taken his pleasure, maybe at the very same time, a man took a beating and died. How's that for sound-proofing, gentlemen? And now Hawley would charge in, the lab crew with him, his little mouth dripping slurs. Maybe he'd pull him off the case. Maybe he'd appeal to the Yard. Fine prospect, either way. He said, "Shit," under his breath.

The walk to Doggett's door was stone. No footprints there. There'd be no footprints anywhere unless the killing was done after the rain.

Goodman opened the door, stood aside, and let the others in, Perkins first.

Doggett's body sprawled on the floor, fragments of bone showing in the blood of his head. Perkins stepped to it and bent down, looking at what he didn't want to see. "Couldn't be deader," he said, straightening.

The spurtle lay on the floor, bloody at the big end, cracked at the handhold. Some hairs sprouted from the blood. On a counter beside the kitchen sink were two small plates, one with a piece of bun on it. A chair lay overturned near the body. Doggett had probably fallen from it, tipping it over as he went down.

"Have to wait," he announced. "Doctor first, lab crew, photographer, the whole damn bunch, but you know that. Come on. Get out. No fingerprints." They knew that, too.

A few people were gathered outside. "What's doing?" one of them called. "What's the matter with Doggett?"

In the group Perkins saw Charlie Evans, the newsman to whom he'd made a promise. "All right, all of you, and you, Evans, Doggett's dead, his head beaten in. That's all we know."

Evans dared to ask, "Any connection with the Smith murder, Inspector?"

"We don't know, and in your boots I wouldn't guess. Now," he went on, "we're sealing the place. Understand? No one can go in. Rendell, stay at the door until relieved. Sergeant Goodman will be back to seal it. Then it's door to door for him. Not you. You stay."

The three of them walked back to the incidents room

where Goodman picked up a kit and then left. Perkins said, hearing himself sigh, "Now for headquarters." He lifted the phone. Then, "Superintendent Hawley? Inspector Perkins here. Constable Doggett's been killed. Head beaten in. That's what I said, and that's all we know. We just found the body. I know, sir. Of course we haven't meddled. Everything is just as it was. Yes, we'll be expecting you."

He hung up the phone and turned back to Charleston. "That's that. Prepare for the royal visit. Where were we?"

"Doggett knew his killer."

"Plain enough from the plates, the half-eaten bun. But, hell, Doggett knew everybody."

Charleston asked, "Did Doggett have any relatives?"

"None close, I think. Have to find out. None around here at any rate."

Charleston lighted a cigar and said through the smoke, "Two murders, and you think of connections."

"Right. Might be, might not be." Perkins paused and went on, "Maybe Doggett found out too much."

"Wouldn't he have told us?"

"Who knows? He might have wanted to show us up, dumb as he was. Improve his image."

Goodman entered then, saying, "Something, maybe."

As if just now conscious of the kit bag in his hand, Goodman put it on top of the file case.

"Sit," Perkins told him.

Goodman sat. "There's a retired constable lives three doors up from Doggett's place. Retired just before Doggett took over. He hadn't heard anything last night, didn't know about the killing until I told him. He said Doggett didn't have an enemy in the world. Then he thought some more and told me a man Doggett had fought with and got convicted had just been released after six months. Word was he'd returned to a little patch of land he owns out of town. His name's Harold Peck."

"The ex-constable?"

"Sam Bailey. He wanted to talk, but I had enough, felt I better report what I had."

Perkins gave himself a minute to consider. "Chick," he said then, "you want to go with Goodman on follow-up? See Bailey, see the man Peck? I'm stuck here."

"Sure."

"If it's a fizzle, maybe you can drive on to Burford and see Burroughs." He consulted his watch. "Should be time enough."

"Yep."

"Then hurry back, will you? I want you on hand if something breaks."

Charleston nodded and followed Goodman out the door.

They walked to the house Goodman had visited. "Lives with his daughter," Goodman said before rapping at the door. A woman let them in, saying with a gesture, "Pa's in the kitchen, having his tea."

A man sat alone at a table, sipping. He was a round man, round and rosy of face and round in body. Charleston was reminded of Santa Claus.

"Hello again, Sergeant," he said, getting to his feet. "Who's your friend?"

"Charles Charleston, an American helping us out."

"I'm Bailey, Sam Bailey," he said, extending his hand. "Seems I heard about you. Sit down, both of you. Tea?"

They sat down at the table after shaking their heads. Bailey took a sip from his cup. "I go to beer when the pub opens," he told them, smiling as if for approval. "So George Doggett got done in? Know anything more than that?" He was asking Charleston.

"Very little. The lab may bring out more. We're waiting meantime."

"Waiting and chatting," Bailey said, smiling again.

"And hoping you can tell us more about Doggett and the man Peck. How well did you know Doggett?"

"Like a grown man knows a boy. Green for the job of constable, he was, green like grass. That's what first got him into trouble. Reminds me of a poem maybe you've heard.

"There is a man in our town
Who often beats his wife,
And any man who beats his wife
Deserves to lose his life."

"I'm afraid I don't follow," Goodman said.

"Too young, maybe. But I tell you, you go to arrest a wife-beater, and the wife will turn on you and try to claw your eyes out and you got two fighters to attend to. That's what George didn't know."

Bailey got up, refilled his cup and sat down again. "I mind it well."

"We're listening," Charleston told him.

"You see," Bailey replied, expanding, "there was a no-good bloke named Harold Peck. He inherited a tiny plot of ground about a mile from the village. It had a hut on it and a couple of ramshackle dumps that passed for buildings. He raised some chickens and once in a while a pig and sometimes hired himself out. He wasn't much of a worker."

"And he's the man Doggett jailed?" Charleston said, hoping to bobtail the story.

Bailey may not have heard him. "Well, there he was, living poor and complaining, whining so much about being hard up that he won the name Poverty Peck. Yes, that was him, but we didn't think he was dangerous. Can't really believe it yet, I can't."

They waited, and he sipped at his tea and smiled again. "No, we didn't think he was dangerous, but one day his little girl came pounding in to tell Doggett her pa was beating her ma to death. Doggett went to see. The fight had ended when he got there, but the woman was lying on a pad, beat up. Peck was just cursing around, and when Doggett tried to arrest him, he put up a fight. And almost before he knew it, the woman was on him, swinging a stick, clawing at his face. Doggett told me afterwards he thought he was fighting for his life. But, by God, sir, he brought them both in and locked them up. The ladies of the village undertook to find a home for the girl."

"Did Peck threaten Doggett, I mean after he was jailed?"

"At the trial and right afterwards he did. Yes sir. He swore he'd get even. Funny thing happened. A Gloucester reporter came, and the Pecks told him Doggett had come and tried to arrest them on some trumped-up charge, and when they tried to assert their rights, he started punching. There were fools who believed the newspaper story. It didn't go over in court, though. Peck got six months and his wife a suspended sentence."

"And they're back at their place now."

"He is, so I hear." He shook his head. "I can't tell you about her."

"I think we've heard all we need to," Charleston said, "but how about directions to the Peck place?"

Goodman got out a pad and took them down. They thanked Bailey, who said, "No thanks called for. My thanks for coming. Not often I get to say so much."

Outside, they found it was raining, not heavily, but the sky threatened more. "Step back inside, sir," Goodman said, "and I'll run and bring the car back."

"No dice, Sergeant. I'll run with you."

Once inside the police car, Goodman said, "Plastic macs in back if we need them."

"We might. It's raining harder."

"Farmers' delight," Goodman said, and turned on the wipers after the car was rolling. The rain started to sheet. He turned the wipers to full speed and squinted through the glass. "In Montana what would you do with so much water?"

"Get out the lifeboats and cheer."

Goodman kept squinting, "Have to watch close. I think we're almost there. Yes." He turned off the paved road into a gravel lane.

A hundred yards or so farther on, Charleston looked down on a small, flooded hollow where three tiny buildings lay in decay. One of them looked to be a dilapidated shack or hut. The others were drooping sheds. A dreary place, depressing, not in keeping at all with what he'd seen of the Cotswolds. The three buildings might tumble in on themselves under the beat of the rain. There was no sign of life, no dog, no cat, no human being, nothing. Just an ocean of mud with wreckage in it.

"Quite an estate," he said aloud to himself.

Goodman parked the car where the mud seemed least. He hopped out, opened the trunk and came back, wet, with two raincoats. As they struggled into them, the door of one of the sheds opened halfway, and a man stood there, peering at them through the rain.

"Shall we slosh over there and question him?" Goodman asked.

"I doubt there's shelter for the three of us in any of those holes. Let's wait a bit. It may ease up, and he's not going anywhere."

"I guess I could drag him over here."

"Just wait."

They sat silent, willing the rain to stop. The man drew back into the shed and closed the door after himself. The rain dwindled. In five minutes it stopped.

"Now?" Goodman asked.

"I reckon. Goodbye, shoeshine."

"More like goodbye shoes."

"Let's roll up our pants a turn or two."

Pants rolled up, they stepped out in mud up to their ankles. They plodded to the door the man had closed. Charleston called out, "Mr. Peck. Harold Peck. Police. We want to talk to you."

The answer came in a high whine. "Get off my property."

"Open up."

"Go to 'ell."

"Open up or we come in."

The door swung open then, hanging crooked by one hinge. Peck stood in the opening with a pitchfork in his hands, its tines pointed out. "Try anything, I run you through." His mouth was wet with spit. He made a small outward jab with the fork.

"You'll do nothing of the kind," Charleston told him. He took a step forward.

"Careful, sir. Careful," Goodman said from just in back of him.

"You know what jail is," Charleston said. "Prison's worse. Give me that fork or that's where you go."

"No. Watch out."

"Give it to me."

Peck retreated a step. "Give it to you, and after you done what you did? Put me in jail. Took me away from my wife. And where's my little girl? That's 'ow you blokes treated me."

"Constable Doggett's dead, Peck. Murdered."

"Doggett kilt? I don't believe you." The news numbed him. He let Charleston take the fork from his unresisting hands.

"His head was beaten in. That's why we're here."

"You're puttin' me on." Peck sucked in a breath as if he hadn't breathed in some time. " 'oo done it? When was it? Where was it done at? It's like I won't believe you unless you say."

"Last night. At his home. That's why we're here." As he spoke, Charleston rested the fork against the wall.

"Jesus God," Peck said, throwing his hands up. "And you think I done it." The narrow shoulders slumped. Charleston hadn't noticed before how small a man he was. No man looked small who pointed a pitchfork at you.

"You hadn't heard about Doggett?"

" 'ow would I? I stick close here, lone-like, not botherin' a soul."

Goodman stepped up beside Charleston. "But you threatened to get him at the time of your trial. Remember that?"

Peck's hands came out in pleading. "A man's like to say a right bunch of things when he's upset. I said I'd get him, but that was just gas and bile. Me get him? Hah."

"Why did you come back here?"

"It's my 'ome. I own it. My old ma left it to me. Where else would I go?"

"Someplace you're not known, I'd recommend."

"I got a good enough name around here. I'm just livin' quiet and waitin'."

Goodman asked, "Waiting for what?"

"My woman, that's 'oo. She went to 'er mum's."

"She's coming back?"

"She's my wife, ain't she?"

"After you beat her up?"

"Some says I did. Some says I didn't. Right or wrong, we get along."

Charleston broke in. "Where were you last night?"

"Right 'ere at 'ome."

"Can you prove it? Did anyone see you?"

"No, not 'ere, but nobody seen me anyplace else. There's your proof."

Charleston looked at Goodman, who shook his head and said, "Stick around, Peck."

"I ain't goin' no place."

At the car they cleaned their shoes as best they could, using sticks and a couple of rags Goodman found in the back.

Goodman said, shaking his head, "You walked right into that hayfork."

"Aw, I figured it was safe enough."

"Meanest weapon on earth. Gives me the shivers. But what about Peck? What's your notion?"

"I'm not counting him in or out, but I don't think he's much of a suspect. A long shot, at best."

"I'm with you. Just an outside chance. He's a bite-if-cornered type, and he'll stay put if we need him. Any other place, and he wouldn't know where to hang his hat."

Goodman started the engine.

Chapter Sixteen

It was one-thirty when Goodman wheeled into Burford and parked at the side of the Lamb Inn. He sat for a moment, not moving to get out. "I've been here once before," he said. "A nice place, not showy. It's older than time."

"I imagine it has its following."

"Yes, sir. Just its age interests a lot of people, and I don't quarrel with that."

"Old alone isn't enough for me."

"Begging your pardon, I know I've seen only a little of Americans, but it seems to me they want everything up to date."

"Not quite that. Sure, we like comfort. Who doesn't? And I like nice-looking things, things with some style to them. I like them first for themselves alone. Maybe our eyes see differently. We're a young country, pretty young for fixed attachments to history. There. I've spoken my piece, and excuse me."

Goodman grinned. "I guess I'm ready to do that. Time to go in, isn't it?"

They entered the modest doorway. On the left was a small

bar and on the right a lobby that looked more like a sitting room. A little fire flickered in the fireplace, and a man sat alone in an easy chair. They walked toward him over an uneven stone floor.

He rose when he saw them, a professional man sure enough, staid as a Barclays bank, with a head of white hair, carefully combed, and a dark three-piece suit. Charleston guessed him to be close to sixty.

Goodman approached him, saying, "I'm Detective Sergeant Goodman, Mr. Burroughs." They shook hands. "And here with me is Charles Charleston, the American I believe the inspector told you about."

"Yes, indeed," Burroughs said, taking Charleston's hand. "And where is the inspector?"

"Tied up, Mr. Burroughs. We've had another murder. The town constable."

"Dear me, what's happening in Upper Beechwood? Murder after murder."

"That's why we're here."

"So I presumed, though I can't see how I can help." He waved a hand in dismissal. "Let it wait for now, please. It's well past noon, and I have ordered beer and some lunch."

"We really haven't time. . ."

Burrough's hand came up, palm out. "Now. Now. When you're on a diet regimen, as I am, you try to eat at the appointed times. There's plenty of time to talk after our food."

As he spoke, a girl came forward with beer. She set the mugs on a table and said, "I'll be right back with the rest."

"Let's move to the table," Burroughs suggested.

The girl reappeared with a tray of sandwiches, some of chicken, others of ham.

Goodman bit into a sandwich and, apparently deciding he had to bide his time, said, "Mr. Charleston is an officer of the law himself. That's in the state of Montana."

"I've heard something about Mr. Charleston," Burroughs

said. "Aren't these sandwiches good? Whenever I'm in Burford, I come here. The inn is so old, so hauntingly old. How
many thousands of people have trod these stone floors? A
man loses himself in the past."

When the sandwiches were gone and the beer down to the
last swallows, Burroughs said, "Now then. You know I've
been expecting you, in fact before now."

"We slipped up there," Goodman said.

"All right, gentlemen. I'm at your disposal, subject, of
course to certain constraints, if, indeed, any now exist."

Charleston thought perhaps a little law-library dust may
have been disturbed by his nodding.

"We don't want you to strain any professional relation-
ships," Goodman assured him. "I'm sure Mr. Charleston
agrees. He's standing in for Inspector Perkins today."

"Surely," Burroughs said, "though it seems a bit shameful
to disturb the peace of this place with talk about killings."

Charleston cleared his throat. "Yes, sir. Now we're wondering whether the two killings were connected, but our
interest here is the murder of Oliver Smith. He was a British
subject who lived in America. No doubt you've heard he was
stabbed to death in his bed."

"All that is known to me, Mr. Charleston."

"You were registered at the Ram's Head Inn at Upper
Beechwood the night of the murder. We have reason to
believe you were there to consult with Mr. Smith, your
client."

"A very nice summation, Mr. Charleston. Please lay any
doubts at rest. I was indeed there, and he was my client."

"And the subject was an estate near Lower Beechwood. He
was laying claim to a share of it?"

"There is no need for you to relate these circumstances,"
Burroughs said with a trace of a smile. "Let me explain."

"I am glad to."

"Fine. Mr. Smith got in touch with me while he was still in

America. He was the survivor, the husband, of a woman named Hannah Hawthorne Smith, who had died recently and left quite a sizable estate to their one child, a son now twenty-two years old. As the widower, he contended he had some rights to the decedent's property."

"She had never remarried?"

"Neither of them had, I was informed. It was a voluntary separation, not a legal one."

"And you took the case?"

"I suppose it is moot and that I may talk about it now that he's dead."

"A sister of his survives."

"I'm aware of that. A Mrs. Post. Mr. Smith talked a bit about her. He also talked about making a will, but delayed it, presumably waiting on the outcome of his claim. He didn't ask me to draft one."

Burroughs went on, "I haven't heard from her and wouldn't represent her if I did. The case was shaky enough as it was."

"You mean you didn't expect to win it?" Charleston asked.

"Expect is a strong word, Mr. Charleston. Let us say I had some hope. On the chance, however, of an amicable settlement out of court, I went to see the boy, Thomas Smith."

They waited for him to continue.

Mr. Burroughs shook his head. "I was sorry afterwards that I did. That young man was impossible. At the very thought of parting with any bit of the estate, he practically frothed at the mouth. He actually threatened me. He made threats against Smith, his own father, if he were ever to meet him." Burroughs sighed. "I came away and prepared the papers."

"Then Oliver Smith came to England and got in touch with you?"

"And asked for a conference."

"And when did you hold it?" Goodman asked.

"After your telephone call I refreshed my memory, or, rather, I consulted my records. I saw him on the night of April twenty-one, a Monday."

"That was the night of the murder, Mr. Burroughs."

"There is no need to remind me, though I didn't find out about his death until later."

"When did you meet him?"

"At nine o'clock that night. I had a dinner invitation at the country home of an old friend — he delayed me. But the late date was quite all right with Mr. Smith."

"How long were you in conference?"

"Possibly an hour. We agreed he should sue for the spouse's full share of the estate, though there was scant hope we'd get that much — not too much hope for anything in my judgment. But he insisted."

"Where did you meet?"

"In my room at the inn."

"And when you were done, what then?"

"I think you are wondering if I went to the bar. I didn't. The pleasures of alcohol, except for an infrequent beer, have long since been denied me. I went to bed, having to be in London in good time the next morning." Mr. Burroughs smiled indulgently. "I imagine you are flirting with the possibility that I killed Mr. Smith. A vain speculation, gentlemen. Of course I didn't. It was to my interest that he remain alive. Solicitors are not in the habit of doing away with their clients."

"You will understand, Mr. Burroughs, that we must ask these questions, even though they seem unnecessary to you."

"I have some familiarity with police procedure." Mr. Burroughs seemed not at all perturbed.

"Were you disturbed at all during the night, by noises, voices, sounds of disorder? There was a fight in the bar that night."

"I heard nothing. I slept without once waking up. I rose

early, checked out, and may already have been back in London before Mr. Smith's body was found."

Charleston, his questions asked, deferred to Goodman, who said, "You told us your hopes of winning in court were not high. Would you be good enough to say why?"

"Does it help, or would it help, your investigation at all?"

"Perhaps not. I'm not sure, Mr. Burroughs, but it might."

"I can tell you. Nothing is really secret now, I believe. Let me start by saying the law seeks reasonable solutions. That is implicit in all the provisions. We function under the act of April one, nineteen seventy-six."

Charleston was tempted to blurt out, "April Fool's Day."

Burroughs went on to explain the law. Why was it, Charleston wondered, listening to him drone on, that attorneys came to life only when facing a jury?

At last the man came to some answers to the question. "At any rate my case was rather weak. For one thing, Mr. Smith, it seemed plain, was a man of some financial substance. That would have been brought out at the hearing. Was it reasonable, then, that he be granted still more?"

"Not to reasonable men," Goodman answered.

"More than that, he had not contributed to the support of his wife or his son. I say not contributed, though early on he tried to. He soon gave up."

"Wasn't there anything to be said for him," Charleston asked, "except that he was the widower?"

"Oh, yes. We weren't quite without ammunition. The wife, according to Smith, was a virago, an entirely impossible woman. Once he had sired a son for her, she had no further use for him, none at all. She ordered him out of the house, out of her sight. Once she threatened him with a knife. Twice, in his early time in America, he had sent checks for the support of the boy. They were never cashed. For a time he tried by phone to get word of the boy. She would slam the receiver."

"Where does reason enter then?" Charleston asked.

"That's the question," Burroughs replied. "Or that would have been the question. Moot now."

"One last question, Mr. Burroughs," Charleston said. "Do you — did you — consider young Smith capable of murder?"

Burroughs considered. "In my experience anyone is if provoked enough. But my impression, vague enough, is that Smith is much bark and little bite."

"No more questions from me, Mr. Burroughs. Sergeant Goodman? No. Our thanks, sir."

They went to the car. "Nice old gentleman," Goodman said as they walked.

"Yes, but we ought to see that Smith boy now. He's hot on my list."

"Right, but we can't. Orders."

"Oh, I'd forgotten."

"Get back as soon as you've talked to Burroughs. That's what Inspector Perkins said."

"He's the boss."

"It's more than that with me, sir. That goddamned Hawley, not fit to wipe Inspector Perkins's boots." Goodman shook his head, as if shaking the words out. "What next? How long before . . .? I don't know. Silly, but could be I can help. Hang together, you know. Anyhow, I can be there."

Chapter Seventeen

AT THE OUTSKIRTS of Upper Beechwood, Goodman said suddenly, "Look, there's the specialty food van! You know, that Peter Tarvin's."

"I see, there by the bed and breakfast place."

"No mistaking it, once you see it. But he won't be having breakfast, not at this hour."

"Maybe just staying in. Special arrangement."

Later, as they neared the inn and the incidents room, Goodman said, "I see God's holding court all right."

Hawley's Rover, unmarked, blocked the beginning of the path to the incidents room. "Polite bloody bastard," Goodman said under his breath. "The king can do no wrong."

Between the Rover and the cottage, a group of men was gathered. Cameras and microphones told who they were.

"So now it's the press," Goodman went on. "They'll be onto you, sir." He moved around the car toward them. Charleston followed.

"What goes on, you officers?" one yelled at them. "Got a suspect yet?" He and the others pressed closer. "Look, the

American! Yank, got anything for us? How do you like playing bobby?"

The man held a mike up to Charleston's mouth. Cameras clicked and lights flashed. "I like it fine," Charleston said into the mike while he grinned at the group. "I'm getting an education."

Goodman undertook to shoulder his way to the door. A reporter blocked him. "Aw, come on, Officer. Be a sport. What's going on?"

"Sorry. Not ours to say. All right, one bit of news if you haven't been told. Constable Doggett was killed with a spurtle."

"What's a spurtle?"

"Look it up."

Goodman leading, they pushed through to the door. They got inside with the voices following them.

Superintendent Hawley sat in Perkins's chair, Perkins at his side. Before them a man waited. He seemed uneasy. Rendell was in the rear.

Hawley looked at them without welcome, as if resenting the interruption. He grunted and said, "Find yourselves seats." Implicit in his tone was the command to keep silent.

"All right. Let's proceed." He spoke to the waiting man, who wore work clothes and had a seasoned and open face and hair that needed cutting. "You were saying your name's Cantrell, Albert Cantrell, and you have no fixed address."

"That's right."

"Explain, please."

"I just got a job in Lower Beechwood. There's a brewery there, and I'm an old hand at it. Go to work Monday."

"So where are you staying?"

"I can't find a place for me and my missus in Lower Beechwood yet, so I'm putting up at my brother's here in the village."

"Your brother's here?"

"Him and his wife took off for London. A treat, like, it was, seeing as how I would be here to see to the house."

"Why didn't you come to the door earlier when you heard the bell ring?"

"You see, I got a little room in back and, being a stranger, it wasn't my business who came to the door."

"But you gave yourself away anyhow, when you let yourself be seen?" Hawley's smile was nearer a sneer.

"Yeah, the constable seen me when I went to the front room to see had I left my pipe in there." Cantrell was answering readily enough, but there was a sort of wariness in his face. No wonder, considering Hawley's speech and manner.

"In the beginning you told us you saw a van. That was after dark last night?"

"You're right, it was."

"Did you notice anything else? Any sign of trouble? Any people about?"

"Not that I seen."

"That was behind the Doggett place?"

"More or less, I guess. Kind of, I would say. But why I know it was the Doggett place is because you said so."

"Never mind that." Hawley moved in his chair. "Perkins, you have anything on your mind? Spit it out if you do."

"Yes, sir. I have some questions."

Hawley didn't look pleased.

"Mr. Cantrell, you have said you parked your car in the rear of your brother's place and there was another car nearby. Is that correct?"

"Just a little wrong. You can call my old job a car if you want to, but it's just loose bolts and nuts and, like I already said, the other machine was a van, not a car. It was a prettied-up van."

"Is it still there?"

"No sir, I went to see."

"Did you take any special notice of it when you saw it last night?"

"Just one thing. In my headlights I seen it was marked Kingston and Heath, Specialty Foods."

"We know that van, Superintendent," Perkins said quietly.

It took Hawley a moment to make the connection. Then he lunged forward, "Good God, yes! That's the specialty salesman. That's Tarvin."

"Yes, sir."

"Put a bulletin out on him! Get him in here!"

Goodman came to his feet. "I'll get him," he said.

"You'll get him?"

"Yes."

Hawley said, unbelieving, "I suppose you have him in the boot of your car?"

"No, sir."

"Where then? How?"

"Observation, sir. Simple observation." Goodman turned his back.

"Take someone with you."

The door closed on his words.

Hawley turned and spoke, his lips barely opening, "Your man, Goodman, seems to be getting a little too big for his job."

"Glad you've noticed." Perkins's tone was icy. "He should have been promoted to inspector long ago."

"That's your opinion." Hawley got up abruptly and began pacing the room. He rubbed his hands together. "But that's neither here nor there. Tarvin. I didn't trust him from the first. He's the connection. You can see it. Smith and Doggett."

Charleston raised an eyebrow, though Hawley couldn't see it. He said, "Oh, yes?"

"They jailed him, didn't they? There's a motive."

"Pretty weak, don't you think?"

"Weak or not, it's a motive. I've known men to be killed for less." Hawley quit pacing and looked toward the door. "I wish he'd hurry up. You ought to light a firecracker under your men, Inspector."

Charleston saw the blood beginning to rise in Perkins's face and spoke before Perkins could. "Goodman doesn't waste time. You can bet on that."

"Humph." Hawley paced again.

Five minutes must have passed, then the door swung open. Tarvin entered, followed by Goodman.

Tarvin asked, "Now what, for God's sake?"

"Sit down, and I'll tell you what." He turned aside. "Cantrell, that's all." He flicked his thumb toward the door. Cantrell went out, looking backward once as if to make sure he'd seen and heard right. Hawley's attention returned to Tarvin. "Here's what, since you asked for it. Your friend, Constable Doggett, has been murdered, done in by blows on the head. Wouldn't you like to see him?"

The words seemed to stun Tarvin. When he spoke, it was in a little voice. "Doggett murdered." He let the words sink in. "But I saw him just last night."

"You certainly did. And wouldn't you like to see him today?"

Tarvin ignored the question, if he heard it. "He seemed well enough, and not bothered. Yeah, he seemed happy even, and now he's dead."

"That's not news to you, is it, Tarvin?"

Tarvin sat straighter, as if suddenly jerked from memory. "Yes, it's news to me. Next you're going to say I killed him."

"Didn't you?"

"No, and I resent the question. It's a fool thing to ask."

"Is it? I have some more fool questions."

"Maybe I'll answer. Maybe I won't. Depends on how crazy."

"All right. All right. What time did you see Doggett?"

"I don't know what time, not exactly. Eight-thirty or nine o'clock. I stayed longer. We drank some beer I brought."

"How much longer?"

"Maybe eleven."

"Then you went home?"

"To where I was staying. I'd called earlier so's they'd expect me. They know me there."

"Any witnesses to that? Anyone see you there?"

"I don't think so. The house was dark."

"So we have only your word for it?"

"My word's good. You can believe that or not, but it's good. Ask anybody."

"How is it you were still there today, in late afternoon?"

"I don't work on Saturday. Poor day for sales. The people at the house knew I wanted to sleep in."

"I see, and that's just by the way. But now, how is it that you called on Doggett last night?"

"He's a friend of mine, or was one, and more a friend than ever after he spoke up for me after that first man was killed. Younger than me, but a friend."

"Yes, go on."

"Now you wait a minute." Tarvin put out a warning finger. "I got a few questions myself, like how was Doggett killed?"

Hawley made a mouth out of what he had for a mouth. "I'll assume for the moment that you really don't know. His head was beaten in with a spurtle. You know, don't you, what a spurtle is?"

"God's sake." Tarvin pulled in a breath and spoke as he blew out. "God's sake. There was one lying loose on the counter last night."

"You knew it for what it was?"

"My mother was a Scot. When she wasn't cracking crabs with it, she was using it to prop up a window or stir the porridge."

"So you admit you saw it?"

"No admitting to it. There it was, like I told you. And that's what killed him?"

"You have it wrong, Tarvin. A person killed him. The spurtle was the instrument." Hawley seemed to like the distinction.

Tarvin said, "Chicken shit."

A banging came at the door, and voices sounded outside. Goodman got up, poked his head out and turned to announce, "The press again."

"Tell them to be patient. Tell them I'll see them before long."

Goodman did so and returned to his chair.

Hawley said, "I'll ask again, Tarvin, why did you call on Doggett?"

"I told you he was my friend. Besides, I had a couple of little treats for him. I knew he loved Bath buns, so I brought him some."

At Charleston's inquiring look, Perkins said in a quick aside, "Sweetened bun. Sugar lump inside."

Hawley fiddled with a pencil. "So that's what you do, peddle food?"

"Oh, right. Can't you see me? I got a pack on my back and a stick in my hand. You want to buy a fine tin knife, Mr. Superintendent, sir?"

"Don't get your back up. Just answer me."

"I sell specialty food, the very best. Some of it I take orders for, some of it I sell out of the van, and I distribute samples."

"A trifling question, but what's this food that's so special?"

"Uncommon jellies and marmalades, not to mention honey. Biscuits like no others you can find. Spiced and pickled goods, and never a complaint about that. Makes a man drool to mention them. That's just a few. And there's Scottish shortbread. You may think you've tasted it, but you won't think so after you've sampled ours."

"I hope that terminates your spiel," Hawley said, sighing on purpose.

"Why, sir, you asked for it," Tarvin answered, with a little nod of apparent satisfaction.

Hawley fiddled with the pencil some more. "You do what you do for a living, I suppose?"

"That's a fool question — what else would I do it for?"

"It's your only source of income?"

"Just what are you getting at?"

"Never mind. Be good enough to answer."

"Can't hurt, I reckon. So it isn't as if my mum and I would starve if I didn't work. We got something laid by or, more like it, something was left to us."

"How much?"

"Now that is none of your bloody business."

"Maybe it is. Maybe it isn't. Just why do you work if you don't have to?"

"Because I like to. Because I don't fancy being a layabout and drawing on savings. And I'd probably drink myself dead if I didn't keep busy. Now what else?"

"No more questions, I believe. Just some possibilities to consider, one of them being that you killed Doggett."

"That won't get you anyplace. I can tell you that."

"Another consideration is motive. Because you were jailed by Smith and Doggett, you might have it in for both. Small resentments can fester."

"Any more dreams, Mr. Superintendent?"

"Naturally. Let's suppose that Doggett knew you had means beyond your job."

"What if he did?"

"Let's suppose then that he knew far more about the knifing of Oliver Smith than he ever told. Let's suppose you killed the man, and that Doggett knew it, and thinking of blackmail, kept that information to himself."

"I don't believe it. You're crazy."

"To sum up, Tarvin. You were on hand when Mr. Smith was stabbed, not only on hand, but fighting drunk, and he helped

subdue you. You couldn't stomach that, could you? Oh no, you
had to get even. You said you didn't do him in. Drunk and out
of it, you said. In jail, indeed! But were you? Were you?"

He waved Tarvin's protest away. "And now this. On hand
again when murder's been done. A friend of the dead man,
you say. Some friend. Some friend. Doggett had something
on you, and there was the spurtle, and wham!"

"By God! By God!"

"We'll let you think about it, twenty-four hours to think
about it, refresh your memory. Then, perhaps, you'll want to
acknowledge your sins."

"Jail me, you mean?"

"What else?"

Tarvin lunged to his feet, leaned across the desk, his hands
tightened into fists, and shouted into Hawley's face, "You
can't do this! Not to me."

Hawley didn't draw back by so much as an inch. Charleston
gave him credit for that if for nothing else. Hawley said,
"You'll find out I can."

Tarvin wheeled around to the others. "Tell him he can't.
I'm an innocent man. He can't."

"You can be held for twenty-four hours, Mr. Tarvin,"
Perkins told him quietly. "If a formal charge isn't made by
then, you go free."

Hawley got to his feet. "Sergeant Goodman, lock the man
up. Here's Doggett's keys." He tossed them onto the desk.
"Give Tarvin a receipt for his things."

Goodman had risen. He walked forward and put a hand
on Tarvin's arm. Tarvin drew back from Hawley and stood
straight. "All right, Sergeant. Not your doing." He swung
his attention back to Hawley and said through his teeth,
"Twenty-four years in jail, Mr. Superintendent, and you still
wouldn't realize what a horse's ass you are."

Hawley smiled his smile. When two men had gone, he said,
"Now there was an interview, Inspector Perkins. Bear down

on them, that's my motto. Mr. Tarvin will sing a different song after he's had time to reflect."

"Shit!"

"What's that?"

"Sure."

"Iron out the details. I'm off. Couldn't really spare the time I've given you." He opened the door. "Headquarters thinks I can be two places at once, two places or more."

A minute after he had gone, Goodman returned.

Perkins said, "Come on, Sergeant." He got up, full of business. "You know where Tarvin was staying?"

"Yes, sir."

"That's more than Hawley does. Come on. Chick, hold down the fort."

Charleston hadn't put the newspaper aside when they returned. "The people he's staying with know Tarvin," he announced before sitting down. "Known him a long time. He's stayed with them before and now he's forced to since the Ram's Head won't admit him after that drunk. They verified what he said, even heard him come in last night, and spoke well of him in spite of his occasional sprees."

He seated himself. "I'm turning Tarvin free. Right now."

"Begging your pardon, sir," Goodman told him. "I doubt you should do that."

"Why, for God's sake?"

"I was just thinking — hasty action could count against you. Hawley would try to make something of it. A few hours more won't hurt Tarvin."

"You telling me to be cautious?"

"Yes, sir."

Perkins seemed to relax and smiled indulgently. "For a little while then, Sergeant. For a little while."

Chapter Eighteen

INSPECTOR PERKINS SAT in his part of the Doggett premises, hardly daring to hope that Drusilla Witt would visit him again tonight. It had been a wearing day — Doggett's murder and with it the doctor, the fingerprint men, the photographers, the questions, and the reports. And don't forget Superintendent Hawley, who was so sure he had found his man. Or was he sure or just hoping? Square-head Hawley, last of the storm troopers.

He sipped at his glass of whisky. Single malt, the only kind worth drinking. Another glass and maybe his mind would quit churning, quit thinking about the day, quit thinking about Charleston's departure. Chick's time was nearly up, or perhaps already up for that matter, and he was fudging his leave just to be helpful.

Rose and Smith and their assignations. He had to follow that up. Best, he thought, to see Rose alone. She'd probably be more forthcoming without others present. No note-taking then. Just himself as a sort of confessor.

Another drink, maybe two, to celebrate Hawley's departure. He'd be back tomorrow, but now, thank God, he was gone.

He was about to load his pipe when a knock came at the door. He went, unbelieving, and there she was beyond the opened door. A little smile played on her lips. "I had to come," she said a little breathlessly. "Are you busy? Am I welcome?"

Without thinking, he pulled her inside and kissed her. "I guess I'm welcome," she said and gave him her mouth again. Then she repeated, "I just had to come, Fred."

"Like the flowers in May, that's how you're welcome," he said, releasing her. "Here, let me have your wrap. Sit down."

She seated herself. She had on a light, gray jacket and underneath it a white blouse that buttoned demurely at the throat. Her skirt was dark blue. It didn't matter what she wore, he thought, she was woman first of all, all woman. Even under artificial light her hair was sunshine.

"Have I passed inspection, Inspector?" she asked lightly.

"With high commendation. Can I get you a drink?"

"Yes, please."

She glanced around while he was pouring it and asked, "Aren't you just a little apprehensive, staying right next door to the scene of a murder, so close to where the body must have been?"

"Me? Nervous? Just because a man lay dead next door? No, not me. Say I've no imagination. Police can't afford it. The only dead men who ever hurt anybody were men who passed on diseases like smallpox. Here's your drink."

He took a straight chair and faced her.

"Is there anything new, Fred? Something you haven't made public? And is what I told you helping?"

"It may. But another murder got in the way, so I can't tell you. Nothing new, though. These things take time. But let's not waste our time talking shop."

"Please, Fred, for just a minute. Is it foolish for me to feel a little frightened sometimes?"

"Of what? Drink up and tell me."

"Two people killed, and no idea who did it. So who's next? Logical question, isn't it?"

"I'd say it was more reasonable to believe there's no next to it."

"But you can't really know."

"I can feel sure, though."

"Now, Fred, please be patient." A little frown creased her forehead. "If there's no next to it, there must be a connection between the two murders. One man did them both for reasons we don't know."

"I didn't quite say that. Please, won't you come now?"

"You don't mean to bed? Surely not, sir."

He didn't answer, for she had risen, put down her drink and stepped toward the bedroom.

Even as she was undressing, she kept talking about the case. "If there's a connection, isn't it likely that Constable Doggett learned something about the murder of Oliver Smith and so had to be silenced?"

"Brainy girl," he said, liking her all the more. "That's a possibility, but did you come here to solve the case? That's not my idea."

"It's so mixed up. Anybody could be guilty, I suppose, even Ben Post, and I guess you would include my husband. They're getting tired of this place and talking about leaving."

"They can't."

"Can't?"

"No. Not for the present."

She sat on the edge of the bed, naked save for bra and panties. "I'm not very happy, Fred."

He stopped in the act of slipping off his shorts and looked at her face. Her eyes were on her folded hands, and he saw a look of sadness there that tore at him.

He took off his shorts and went to her and kissed her and said, "You look so troubled. Please don't be. Just come to bed, honey."

Silent, she removed her things and let him cuddle her. And then he was in her again, and all else left his mind. Afterward, with her head on his shoulder, he said, "Now tell me, Dru."

She was crying softly. Before she answered, she wiped her eyes with a corner of the sheet. "I'm thirty-three," she said and paused, and he wondered whether she was traveling those years again. "I was married at twenty, and now I keep asking myself, is this all there is to it? Tell me, Fred, is this all there is to it?"

"You mean to life?"

"Those dreams. Those old dreams. Just to be alive was joyful, and the future so bright. Gay was a good word in those days, and we were gay." Silence again. "Gay with dancing, happy with songs. And ahead, just dazzle. That's enough. I'm maudlin."

"No. Go on." Her body was warm against his.

"Don't you remember the brave days? I know you do. When life was overflowing, and the future was all promise. And it all turns out to be nothing, nothing at all."

Out of impulse he said, "I wouldn't call being together now nothing. I wouldn't call this making love nothing."

She was slow to respond. "No. Not nothing, but not everything either, not what life might be." She halted and went on, "You may think I'm promiscuous, but I'm not. I'm not faithful to my impotent husband, you know that, but I do discriminate. Maybe that's all there is to sex morals, discrimination. With you I discriminated. I knew that you wore your stiff manner over sensitivity. I knew you for a good man, Fred."

"Hasty conclusion."

"No. I knew."

"Thanks, anyway."

"Am I being self-pitying?"

"That's all right."

"I hate self-pity, but here goes. My husband came down

with the mumps right after we were married. He had a hard time. It made him sterile. It didn't make him impotent — that's what the doctors said — but it convinced him he was, and so he was sure enough. His imagination and his fears got the best of him. Still have the best of him, for that matter. He made himself into a eunuch."

She gave a little laugh, not of amusement. "I was all sympathy until I found out he didn't want a wife anyhow. He wanted a personal adornment, something to show off to the fellows with possessive pride. Vanity, that's what it was, though impotence might have had a little something to do with it. He could brag, not in words, of course, 'See here, men, what I have.' I was more of a something in those days."

"That's hard to believe." He put a hand on her breast.

"I'm not through." She was speaking with more vigor. "He never wanted a wife, never wanted a companion, never wanted someone close and confiding, someone to confide in himself. He wanted a doll."

"He's a fool."

"No. He's just himself. Do you think I know anything about his business, really anything about him, what he does, what he plans, where he stands in the world? All I know is, and this from the way he spends it, is he makes money." She gave a little snort. "Money! Jesus, Fred, I want a life."

She was crying again. He wiped her tears with the corner of the sheet, and all at once she seized him and brought him onto her, and he had time to think that grief and sex were close companions before all thoughts vanished, until only the now was here.

Afterward, lying there spent, she said, "Fred, do you suppose . . ."

"Not until you tell me."

"It's foolishness. It's a holdover dream from when I was young. But is it too late to start over again? I think of Sherwood Anderson. He was an American author. All of a sudden one day he chucked a job he hated and said, 'Here beginneth a new life.' I wish I could say that."

"You're young yet."

"Not so young, but what of it? Well, this, anyhow. If I ever found the right man, I'd say to hell with everything and go with him and not give a damn about trinkets and fashions. Then I wouldn't be asking myself, 'Is this all there is to it?'"

He felt a stillness in him, an edge of surely foolish hope. Old Fred Perkins and this lovely woman. More than fifteen years of difference there, and what did he have to give her aside from the age gap, a modest income, and lonely nights while work kept him from home? And after that first marriage and virtual failure, did he want to be married again? Did he dare, old fool that he was, to commit himself? He said, "My dear," half-choking on the words.

Was this all there was to it? The question repeated itself in his mind while she lay silent by his side. Was this all there was to his own life away from her? Bachelor quarters and bachelor meals and no one to care about except for the casual and heated moment? The grief and scum that a detective met with, and no one at home to talk things over with, no one to come from the kitchen and kiss him when he got home from work. No welcoming voice. No snatches of song. Just his life as it was, and that was all there was to it.

He hugged her convulsively and said, "The right man. You deserve the very best."

She answered, "I think I've found him."

He had that to think about after she'd left.

Chapter Nineteen

CHARLESTON WOKE UP at what he thought was an early hour, so early that few were astir yet. He heard the muted sound of an automobile, a couple of distant voices, and soft and single footsteps in the hall. When he listened, the silence sang in his ears. Then it came to him that the day was Sunday. Church bells would be ringing soon.

Sunday, the so-called day of rest, not observed by policemen. But, for a change, he felt in no special hurry this morning, though Geeta, stirring now, looked at him and said, "You get so intent, Chick. Right now you have that hunter's look in your face."

"Harsh words, girl. I'm a peaceable man."

"Here I was, dreaming about London. And you must have been dreaming about the case."

"You'll feel better after some coffee. Shall I order some up?"

"No thanks."

"Anyhow, you'll see London tomorrow."

She took a long breath before she said, "You mean . . . ?"

"That's what I figured all along. Two days in London for us. You can begin packing up."

"Oh, Chick." Her voice trembled, all vexation gone. "I won't let you do that. Just bow out of the case? Admit defeat? I don't want my two days in London. They're yours."

"No, ma'am."

"Please, Chick?"

"Sorry, dear. There are important things and there are more important things."

She reached for him. He put his arm around her and kissed the soft mouth, thinking again how lucky he was.

He said, "I have today left, and there's young Tom Smith to call on."

"That spoiled pup."

"He could be guilty. He's a lead at least, the only one I can see. Now go back to sleep."

"I might go to church later on. The Episcopal service, or Anglican, is mostly ceremony."

"And you don't want a minister blatting at you?"

"How did you guess?"

He went to the bathroom, showered, shaved and got dressed. He turned to the bed to say goodbye, but she was already asleep, maybe dreaming of London.

He took his time over breakfast and then walked outside to the incidents room, where he found Perkins and Goodman. After greetings, he asked, "Where's Rendell? Nosing around?"

"For what good it might do. He couldn't get any more on the young visitor from the cigarette seller." Perkins took a puff on his pipe and laid it aside. "You'll be pleased to know that the high muckymuck won't be around today." Perkins growled in his throat. "A man of manifold duties, our superintendent. Now it's a killing in Cheltenham." Perkins took another puff on his pipe. "That leaves Tarvin to us."

"And you'll teach him to talk." It was Goodman speaking, derision in his voice.

"That's right. Lean on him. That was Hawley's order. Lean, the devil! Not me. I'll turn him out."

Charleston lighted his morning cigar, got it going properly, and asked, "What else is on the docket, Fred?"

"For me, more waiting. Wait for the pathologist's report, if there is one yet. Wait for word on fingerprints. Try to match them here unless they're on record. Reports to write. Tarvin to see again. I suppose a man's got to expect days like this."

"This is my last shift as helper, if I've been one," Charleston said. "Today ends it, you know."

"Yes, I know. Don't make me think about it. I'll get around to thanking you by and by."

"Not necessary, Fred. Precious little I've contributed."

Goodman broke in, "And I won't ever see you walk into a hayfork again."

" 'Fraid not. Now today, Fred, you being tied up, how about me and young Tom Smith? I'd like to talk to him. There's a chance there."

"Good idea. Sooner we see him the better. Go on, you and Sergeant Goodman both." He managed a smile. "I don't want you around looking doleful."

Charleston took time to ask, "Any word from Washington?"

"Not a peep out of headquarters. Nothing on the lodgers at the inn, either. Takes time, it seems. I hope Hawley isn't sitting on it."

Before they went out the door, they got his parting shot. "Decorations for you both if you get a confession. Stay till you get one, eh?"

It was just as well to have them gone, Perkins thought. Probably better. A private conversation with Rose Whaley was more likely to bring results than an official one, with Goodman sitting in the rear, taking note of everything she said. That would be enough to upset the girl, to stand in the way of a confession of her relations with Smith. Correction: her reported relations.

The telephone rang. Pathologist's preliminary report.

Death from a fracture of the skull. Skull uncommonly thin. No other signs of violence. No symptoms of poisoning. Victim a healthy young man before death. Time of death, approximately 11 to 12 P.M. Full report to follow.

So much for that, he thought as he hung up. No more and no less than he expected, save for the mention of a skull thinner than usual, which he had suspected.

He was glancing at his watch when the telephone rang again. Two good sets of fingerprints, one of Doggett, the other unidentified. Nothing else but blurs. Be sure to take prints of Peter Tarvin.

There was Hawley's fine hand. Yes, take Tarvin's prints. Didn't the numbskull know they were taken as a matter of course when Tarvin was jailed?

It was after ten-thirty. Rose would be finished in the dining room, or just about finished. He'd have to summon her himself. He smiled inwardly, thinking how dependent on Goodman he had become.

He found her in the kitchen, lending a hand with the clean-up. She smiled at the sight of him, then sobered as he beckoned. "Yes, Inspector Perkins," she said, coming to where he stood in the doorway.

"Good morning, Rose. I have just a few more questions to ask. Wouldn't it be well to come out to the cottage? Now don't be alarmed, my dear."

She hung up a dish towel, her hands slow with this little task, and answered, "I can't imagine why, but if you want to, Inspector."

Such a clear day, Perkins thought as they walked to the incidents room, such a lovely and innocent day. He saw that she was seated comfortably before the desk and then went around and took his chair.

"Rose, my dear," he began softly, "you can see that we are alone. No one is on hand to take notes, and I promise you absolutely that nothing you say will go beyond this room unless it becomes vital to the prosecution of a murderer. Do you understand?"

She nodded, her wide eyes fixed on him. He hated to proceed. "Now, then, Rose, I'm afraid you haven't been altogether forthcoming when we questioned you before."

"What do you mean by that?"

There was nothing else for it then, and he let the words come. "We have it on good authority that you and the late Mr. Smith were intimate."

Her chin thrust out. "I found him dead, if that's intimate. I told you that."

"Just that, and nothing more. What took place before you found him? That's the question. It's best that you tell me."

Her hand were working in her lap. Perkins had an absurd impulse to hold them. "I know it's rough, girl. So many things are, but we surmount them and go on. Please tell me about yourself and Mr. Smith."

"You said you had it on good authority. On whose authority, I want to know?" Her expression, as well as the words, demanded an answer.

"I can't tell you. That would be betraying a confidence, and then you yourself would doubt me. But I keep my promises. You can trust me."

Her hands were still working. Out of a wooden face she said, "He raped me."

"He raped you?"

"Took advantage of me. That's better."

"And how did that happen?"

Her words were stiff but distinct, each one slow, almost as if she were writing. "He asked me to bring tea to his room, asking would I do it in person. As soon as I put the tray on the table, he grabbed me and threw me on the bed. I don't have to tell you the rest, only he turned gentle afterwards and offered me five pounds."

"Did you take it?"

"I thought I deserved it, seeing how rough I was used. I was so mixed up."

"I can understand that," Perkins told her. "But there's more, isn't there, Rose?"

The wooden face lost its rigidity. A gush of tears came from her eyes. He went to the bathroom and came back with a cold cloth and said, "Here, girl."

"I'm so ashamed," she said through the cloth. "What will people think of me? What will Auntie say?"

"They won't learn from me. I've promised you that. So you went back to him? You were about to say that. How many times, Rose?"

"I don't know. Three or four."

"Tell me why."

She was shaking her head and still crying. "I couldn't stand it if it got known."

"Was it that you needed money, Rose?"

"No. I refused to take anything."

"After lying with him again?"

A nod was her answer. He waited for more. When she spoke, it was haltingly, like a child owning up to a fib. "I don't know all the why of it. I'm so sinful. I'm so wicked. He made me that way."

"And did you kill him for it?"

An eye looked over the wet cloth. "Kill him! Don't ask such a crazy thing."

She took the cloth from her face and went on, "So why did I do what I did? I didn't know the ways of men and women, and I was . . ."

He spoke for her. "Fascinated."

"Yes, and I didn't know there was such wicked pleasure in the world, such awful pleasure." She shook herself as if to shake off remembrance. Her voice went sad. "I can't hold up my head anymore, not around here."

"Is that the end of the story, Rose, or have you more to tell me?"

A flare of anger came and went out with her words. "You expect more! More? What more? More than this disgrace?"

"Rose," Perkins said, speaking kindly, "you aren't the only one who ever broke the rules. Believe me when I say that. If what you did is such a dreadful sin, then thousands, millions of us, are doomed. I don't think you're much of a sinner, my dear, and I don't think you're ruined. So smile if you can. Face the world. It forgives and forgets and goes its own way. Be brave and go yours."

So much for his role as comforter, he thought. If there was anything more, he had to turn off the sympathy.

"Now, Rose," he said, "if there's anything else, I want to know it. Come clean. That's best for you."

Her voice rose. "Come clean, when I feel so dirty!"

"You want us to spot the murderer, don't you?"

"What good would that do? It won't bring him back."

"As a civilized people . . ."

She leaped to her feet. "Be civilized yourself!"

A choking sob came out of her. She ran to the door, crying out. "There's nothing else. I've owned up to my sins! Isn't that enough for you?"

She wrenched the door open and slammed it behind her.

Missed again, he told himself, sighing. He'd muffed it. She must know more, considering, but how could he get her to tell?

Rendell dodged in. "No local record of Smith's marriage or the birth of a son," he announced.

"County records. Gloucester?"

"Nothing there, either. Sorry. Now what?"

When Perkins didn't answer, he added, "I thought I'd get myself something to eat, sir. Care to join me?"

Perkins thought he might as well. What the hell? He could dig in his mind as well over a meal as here.

At the pub, feeling suddenly hungry, he asked for a steak and kidney pie. Rendell ordered a plowman's. The pie was uncommonly good, made on the premises, not in a factory.

So let the pie ease his mind, as Rendell would say. Let it reveal what he couldn't find. Let it make him forget Hawley and his career and all that. The other customers swam in his eyes, floating dim in the current of his thought.

Rendell waked him by asking, "All through, Inspector?"

As they got up to go, Perkins said, "I have to see the man Tarvin. Will you bring him from the jail? Here's the key."

"Yes, sir."

The constable was prompt. Perkins had barely had time to seat himself in the incidents room when Rendell came in with Tarvin.

Perkins nodded and said, "Sit down, Mr. Tarvin."

"And hear some phony charge, I suppose?"

"Have you anything to add to what you said yesterday? Anything to correct, now that you've had opportunity to think?"

"Not one blasted thing. I spoke the truth and all of it."

"I believe you. There is no charge. You may go — with my apologies."

"What happened to your wolf? Did you cage him?"

"If you mean Superintendent Hawley, he's busy on another case. And by the way, he's not my wolf."

Tarvin got to his feet. "I have a feeling I owe you the apology." He leaned over the desk and offered his hand. "No hard feelings, not against you."

"Thanks. Constable Rendell will return you your things."

When that was done, Tarvin went out, managing a whistle.

Perkins looked at his watch and said aloud, "Wonder what's happening to Charleston and Goodman? They ought to be back before long."

"I don't know, sir," Rendell answered. Of course he didn't know. Foolish question in the first place. Rendell had no idea where or why they'd gone.

The phone rang, and Rendell listened. Perkins said "Yes" into it. Then, "Inspector Perkins here." A silence. "Yes, I let him go. No, I didn't lean on him." Silence. "No, I didn't take his prints. Why? Goddamnit, because we already had them. Goodman took them when he jailed him. Routine, as you ought to know. Charge Tarvin with what we had? With only that, for Christ's sweet sake!" Perkins's voice got hotter as he spoke. "Look, Hawley, I know nothing could please you more than for me to make a fool of myself. But goddamnit, Hawley, I won't. You make a bloody fool of yourself trying to make a fool out of me. You've got a mean mind and nothing much in the way of brains, and to hell with you." A harder bite, an ice-cold one, came into his voice. "You do that, Hawley, and tell the chief constable to expect my resignation along with the reasons for it. Oh, yes, and have a nice day yourself."

As he hung up the phone, settling it with a sort of cold decisiveness, Rendell gave a low whistle not meant to be heard.

Chapter Twenty

IT WAS ALMOST TWILIGHT when Goodman pulled up in front of the Smith place for the second time that day. Ahead of them a parked car shone in the headlights. "Seems our bird's lit," he said. "Chase half over England trying to find him, wait while we grow calluses on our butts, and here the rooster is." There was tired disgust in his voice. "Drives a Bentley. That figures."

"Come on then," Charleston told him.

They walked to the door. The manservant they had talked to earlier in the day answered their ring. He was an older man with a touch of gray in his hair. He had told them that morning that Mr. Smith was out for the day and suggested a few places he might possibly be found.

After they had turned away, Goodman said, "It beats me, him playing bloody butler to a twenty-two-year-old bloke." But neither now nor when they had seen him that morning did the man indicate that he found his position irksome.

"Yes, gentlemen," the man said. "Now if you'll just wait in the hall. And might I have your names, please?"

"Certainly." Goodman gave them to him.

The man disappeared without comment, then reappeared, saying, "This way, gentlemen."

He led the way into a large living room. Charleston took quick note of a green carpet and white walls with small splashes of yellow. The blank face of an oversized television set stared at him. Near it was a stereo. A sideboard too big for its function stood against the facing wall. The other furniture was massive too and, to him, tackily ornate. What was it, late Victorian, that Geeta called this swollen stuff?

The man called their names and withdrew. A boy lounged in an overstuffed chair and didn't get up. A young and rather pretty girl sat on a sofa, her hands smoothing the wrinkles in her red dress. Both young people looked rather steamy.

"Well," the boy said, "what is it?"

Goodman asked, "Your name is Tom Smith?"

"Why ask me if you know it?"

"Simple. To make sure you're the one we want to talk to. We had a time chasing you down. Your man out there had a number of ideas, all wrong, about where you might be."

"He's not a good guesser. Now so far as I know it's not against the law to take your girl to the beach."

"Not lately anyhow. But again, you are Tom Smith?"

"That's me. So what?"

"So now we'll seat ourselves as you so kindly didn't ask."

Goodman pulled up a chair for Charleston and sat on the sofa by the girl. He was showing another side of himself, a competent, take-charge side ordinarily restrained in deference to Inspector Perkins.

"What have I done now?" Smith asked. "Had a wreck? Stolen a pig? Contributed to delinquency? Spit it out."

"My colleague has some questions to ask you," Goodman told him.

Smith turned his head. "Yes. Sure. The famed Yankee sheriff who rides to the rescue. Ask away, man."

Charleston sat forward. "We have reason to think you were

in Upper Beechwood last Monday night, the night your father, Oliver C. Smith, was murdered."

"Where'd you get that? Reading tea leaves?"

The girl stirred and said, "Monday night!" and fell silent, her brow wrinkled.

"So, on the basis of reports, we assume that you were in Upper Beechwood that night," Charleston went on. "For what purpose? Tell us that."

"I wasn't there."

The girl muttered, not as if to support him, "I didn't think he had a girl in Upper Beechwood." She added as if to herself, "Not there."

Charleston held up his hand, "Just a minute, please, miss." He switched to the boy. "One theory is that you flew into a rage and stuck a knife in your father. He was your father. Right?"

The boy cried out, "Don't you speak of my father. Father, my arse! I wouldn't know him if I saw him and if I did, I'd spit on him."

"Why?"

"He deserted my mother. He deserted me. He went to America and made a lot of money, but did we ever see any of it? Not one bloody penny."

"What were you doing in Upper Beechwood, then?"

"I tell you I wasn't there."

"Where were you?"

The girl broke in again. "You weren't at home and you weren't with me — I'd like to know what." She settled back in a quiet ferment.

"Mr. Smith," Charleston said, "there are other questions. We understand that your father tried to claim a part of your inheritance?"

"He did, the son of a bitch! He sent a London solicitor nosing around. I put the run on him. What my mother left is mine, all mine, and no one's entitled to one bloody bit of it."

"Not if he's dead."

Almost unheard, the girl was talking to herself.

"It must have been that Laura."

Charleston went on, "So there's another motive, Mr. Smith. You wanted him dead."

"That's different from killing him."

"But you hated him enough to kill him?"

"I'm just glad he's dead. That's all."

"I still want to know where you were Monday night."

"I'll tell you," the girl burst out of her ferment. "He wasn't at home, and he wasn't with me." Her eyes were on Charleston. "You see, we get together every night. At least we're supposed to. We're going steady. We've even talked about marriage." As if the decision were hers alone, she added, "I haven't made up my mind yet." She would, though, and in the boy's favor, Charleston thought, or in favor of the money.

"I see," he said.

"But last Monday night — I'll never forget it — I waited and waited, and I tried to ring him, and he didn't come by or telephone, not until eleven o'clock, and I put a flea in his ear when he did and hung up the phone."

"You're sure of the time?"

"As sure as I am of my own name. I watched every minute crawl by. It was right at eleven."

"What did you do then, Mr. Smith?"

"When?"

"After she put that flea in your ear?"

"That's not important. My own affair."

"I'll tell you what he did," the girl spoke up. "He got drunk. After eleven o'clock he called me every quarter of an hour. Eleven-fifteen, eleven-thirty, fifteen minutes to midnight. He made his last call at twelve o'clock. He could hardly speak his own name."

"I wish you'd shut up," the boy told her. Then to Charleston, "There's no law I know of against a man taking a drink. Once in a while he takes one too many. There's no law against that, either."

Charleston glanced at Goodman, knowing what was in his

mind. They were barking up the wrong tree, if the girl spoke the truth.

The girl couldn't quit talking. "What was he doing before eleven o'clock, that's my question." Her eyes went to Charleston. "Mr. Tom Smith is such a loving man. Why don't you ask some of his girlfriends?"

Smith said, "You're crazy."

"Crazy, is it? Just say where you were Monday night. I've asked before, and I'll keep on asking. Maybe in time you'll quit being a clam."

"That's nobody's business but mine."

"I'll tell you something, Mr. Tom Smith. Two can play at your game. I'll be pussycat and you keep being tom. That's funny. Spell tom with a capital letter nor not, it means the same thing. Yes indeed. I'm not such an old bag. I can find another friend easy enough."

Smith came to his feet, his face flushed, her anger kindling his own. "You'll wish you hadn't. Now will you shut up?"

"No, I won't shut up. You'd throttle me, is that it?" Her voice was taunting. "What a nice revenge. Just like you, too."

"Not a bit of it. I'd save you for myself, that is if I still wanted you. It's your new boyfriend who'd wish he never set eyes on you."

"Oh my. Oh my."

Charleston broke in, "All right, Smith. Where were you Monday night?"

"Everybody's business, eh? All right. I was playing cards and losing my shirt." Smith sat down again.

The girl asked, "Where?"

"At Paul's Place."

"Low company, and you were drinking, too."

"What if I was? Sure, I was drinking, drinking until they wouldn't serve me any more. Had the nerve to say I'd had enough. I quit the game then. No drink, no play, I told them, and the devil with them. If I wanted a drink, they couldn't stop me. I had plenty of whisky at home."

"So you showed them, yeah, you got back at them." The girl was jeering.

"Lay off, will you? Just lay off."

"And then you drove home drunk."

"Of course I drove home. No accident. I drive just as well with a few drinks as I do cold sober."

"That's what the man said before he hit the tree."

"I got here, didn't I?"

"Hold it now, Smith," Charleston told him. "You came home and drank and then what?"

"I must have passed out, if you have to know."

Goodman broke in, "Was your man here?"

"Must have been."

"Get him in here."

The girl got up and pulled a cord near the window. A bell sounded distantly, and almost before it had ceased, the manservant appeared and said, "Yes, sir."

"These are policemen," Smith told him. "A couple of nosy gentlemen. Be nice and polite, Farney, and tell them what they want to know, even if it's my bathroom habits."

Farney turned, facing Charleston, who asked, "Do you remember Monday night, the night of the twenty-first?"

"Quite well, sir."

"And why is that?"

Farney hesitated, until Smith called out, "Spill it, Farney. Spill it."

Farney's gaze went from Smith's face to Charleston's. "Mr. Smith came home a bit before eleven."

"Drunk?"

"I would hesitate to say he was strictly sober, sir."

"Then what?"

"He asked for a bottle, a glass and some water, and I put them on a table in front of him."

"And?"

"He began drinking. Then he asked for the phone, and I brought it to him. It's movable and plugs in there by the sofa."

"Go on."

"I left him then, thinking there was no more I could do. But I was worried." He turned to Smith. "You'll excuse me, sir, but I had to listen and keep a watch on you."

"Sure. Sure. Go on. Tell the man."

Farney said, looking toward Smith, "I heard your voice several times sir. I assumed you were using the telephone. Then, some time afterwards, I heard the sound of a fall. I hurried in. You were lying in a heap on the floor."

Charleston prodded him. "Say it, if he was. Drunk and unconscious."

"Not quite, sir. He was a bit difficult. He didn't want to move or be moved. I had some difficulty in getting his shoes off. Then I put a pillow under his head and threw a coverlet over him against the cold. He lay there all night. I know. I kept peeking in."

Goodman got to his feet. "He's not worth it, Farney," he said. "Let him go to hell in his own basket."

Farney asked, "Is that all?" When no one answered, he withdrew.

Charleston rose and stepped to the door with Goodman. Sounds of argument followed them into the hall. "So you have a new pastime, do you?" the girl was asking. "Gambling, and did you lose your pants, too?"

"I said to knock it off, knock it off, knock it off . . ."

Goodman closed the door, and they walked to the car. "How'd you like to be married to her?" he asked.

"Or have him for a husband? Evens up."

"High time we got back. No telling what's happened." He put the car in gear. "We might as well have stayed home, or almost."

"Think so?"

"Don't you?"

"I'm not sure."

Chapter Twenty-One

SITTING ALONE in the incidents room, Perkins felt a kind of relief. No more holding back before the sneering allusions, the half-open threats of one Superintendent Cecil Hawley. No more provocations from that tight little mouth he'd so often wanted to batter. If worst came to worst, he supposed he could find something to do, enough to supplement the small pension he'd earned. More likely, though, his superiors, mindful of his services, would think to let him down easy by putting him on a desk. Same difference, though. He'd resign.

So be it. Yet maybe the chief constable would listen to his reasons. He would cling to that possibility without counting on it much. Hawley sucked up to the chief, and the chief was getting old and set in his opinions. Yet there was that slim chance.

It was early evening by now. So where in God's name were Charleston and Goodman? Not that it mattered much, unless they'd come on to something sure-fire. Ah, forget that. Good to be alone and let his mind wander. Rendell had left sometime earlier, tired of this waiting.

He lighted his pipe and let his thoughts drift, and in half an hour Charleston and Goodman came in. "Sorry, sir," Goodman said. "We had a time running Smith down. Then we didn't prove anything except he's out of the picture. Two witnesses to prove it. He was a hot prospect, too." Goodman shook his head ruefully. "It's a letdown, kind of."

"Part of the business, that is, eliminating possibilities. What else?"

Charleston answered him. "Oh, he's Oliver Smith's son all right, though he hates to admit it, but his time on Monday night is accounted for. He stood up his girlfriend — gambling, so he said. Then he went home, drank more, and passed out along about midnight. We have his manservant's word for that."

"That's all? Really?"

"Allowing for a wild hunch I won't mention."

He might as well tell them, Perkins thought. Better tell them right off, the simple facts without self-pity. He said, "We're off this job, all of us."

He saw Goodman's face. He heard Goodman say, "Christ!"

He continued, making his tone easy, "A replacement for me will come in the morning. Until then I suppose I'm in charge, at least nominally."

"So you told the bastard off?" Goodman asked.

"I had that satisfaction, Sergeant. I rather indulged myself."

"I knew you'd do it some time, but . . ." Goodman's voice trailed off.

Out of a small twist of thought, he said, "So, Chick, you aren't alone. It's my last day, too." His smile, he knew, had no amusement in it.

"Yeah. Not a productive day for either of us."

"It got me fired. Hawley would call that productive."

"And nothing else?"

"Wrong, but it doesn't matter now. I brought Rose Whaley

in here for more questions. That was before I told Hawley off. And, don't you know, Rose finally confessed that she and Oliver Smith had been intimate. He as good as raped her the first time, but she went back, fascinated, and learned to like it."

Goodman let out a mere "Oh."

Of a sudden Charleston snapped his fingers and said, "That's interesting."

"Wait a minute now. At the end I insisted that Rose tell me more if she knew anything. She got indignant. She said I had shamed her enough. She got hysterical and flung herself out the door. Something secret there, but how can we make her tell?"

"Could you get her in here again?"

"I suppose. You want more hysterics?"

"Just get her in, if you will."

"It's daft," Perkins said. "But, Goodman . . ."

Goodman was on his feet. He went out, saying, "I'll bring her."

Perkins asked, "Now what is it?"

"It's a hunch. String along, Fred. Play a part. The bad cop and the good cop routine. You know it?"

"Heard of it."

"Let me be a fool, if that's the way it turns out."

"Never a fool, Chick, but maybe on the wrong track?"

"Could be."

Perkins relighted his pipe and had time for a puff before Goodman entered with Rose. "I'm sorry, Rose. It's annoying, I know, but Mr. Charleston wanted to see you. I told him about, well, about what you'd told me."

She let out a stifled cry. "But you said it was confidential!"

"I said it would not go outside this room, and it won't unless absolutely required. We are not gossips here, Rose. We can be trusted."

She folded her hands in her lap, not quite believing. She

pressed her lips tight as if never to open them. Her face showed rigid control.

Perkins nodded to Charleston, and Charleston said, "Miss Whaley, I want to be assured — I should say we want to be assured — that you have told the whole truth."

Through stiff lips she said, "I swear to it."

"And you've held nothing back? Nothing at all?"

She answered with a little spurt of anger, "My God, I've laid myself bare, and you ask me that!"

"I wanted to be sure before proceeding." Charleston hitched around in his chair and said, "There's nothing else for it then, Fred."

Perkins answered blindly, "It seems not."

"Everything points that way." He sighed, taking his time. "The extreme nervousness when questioned. The daily attendance at church."

Perkins understood the reference then, understood it without understanding. He saw the girl's hands tighten in her lap. She was as still and rigid as stone. Good tactics, he reflected. A clever ruse, shrewd if a bit dodgy. Chalk one up for Charleston then, and let him get on with this unpleasant business. It wasn't to his own taste, though — be honest — he would have used it if it had occurred to him.

"It's not pleasant. Hateful but necessary. But there's no choice. We have to charge Mrs. Vaughn with the murder of Oliver C. Smith."

Rose came out of her chair then, her face torn. She shouted, "No! No! Not Auntie!"

"It just shows you never can tell," Charleston said into her cries. "She's probably been praying for forgiveness." The girl kept shouting protests.

Perkins thought he must be in some kind of stage play, hearing lines, saying lines of a drama he didn't know the end of.

"Look," Rose said, stepping toward Charleston, "she goes

to pieces when questioned. She's just naturally nervous. She goes to church every morning. What for? She's praying to live a little longer. And you can't understand!"

"I understand this much, that you're trying to protect your aunt. It won't work."

"You bloody man. You'll kill her. She has heart trouble."

"Too bad."

"But I know Auntie didn't kill him."

"You may know. We don't. Where's the evidence?"

Rose bent her head and shook it back and forth, saying nothing.

"So you haven't got it. All right, Miss Whaley, you may go. Sergeant, will you bring in Mrs. Vaughn?"

Neither of them moved at once. Then the girl went to her chair, collapsed in it, and said, "All right. All right." Her voice was thin now. "You make me choose, but it's hard, so hard." At the end her words were a whimper. She was crying.

Perkins thought it time to intercede. "Rose," he said softly, "Choices are always hard. They leave regrets, and the regrets make us sad. But we have to choose, and we do, praying for the best. We have to take sides sometimes. My dear, tell us how you know Mrs. Vaughn can't be guilty."

"Do I have to?"

"Yes, dear."

"You know about Mr. Smith and me?"

"Yes, you told me."

In a tiny voice she began to speak in short, flat phrases, with pauses between. "I went to see him. It was that night. Afterwards. You know, after love, we were drowsing. Backs to the door. That's how we lay. The light was on, but still we were dozing. He always left the bedside light on." She gulped. "He said it was because he liked to look at me." She paused then, as if for breath to go on. "This is so awful. I lied, too. I lied to get into his room. I told Auntie after work that I was tired and ready for bed.

"We were just drowsing. His arm was around me. All of a sudden his body jerked. He kind of reared up in bed. Then he fell back and was still. I sat up. There was a knife sticking in him, and I knew he was dead."

"What else did you see?"

"I saw the door being closed."

"Who was closing it?"

"I don't know. I couldn't see who it was."

For what seemed a long moment, Charleston looked at her. To Perkins she seemed frail and even younger than she actually was. A young girl in distress with the law barking at her. He could wish Charleston didn't have to go on.

With a slight movement of his head, as if her last answer didn't satisfy him, Charleston changed his tack. "What did you do then?"

"I listened for breathing, I mean his breathing. I felt for a heart beat." The words came in slow and hushed sentences, as though she were doing these dread things again. "He was dead. I could tell that much. It was awful."

"But I believe you didn't sound the alarm right away?"

"I didn't. I couldn't. I got out bed. He had dropped his jacket and trousers on the floor and left his shoes there."

The randy dog, Perkins thought. So eager to jump in bed with the girl that he couldn't wait to get all his clothes off.

Charleston went on, "So he was just partly dressed?"

"Yes."

"Go on, please."

"I put his jacket and trousers on a chair. There was nothing much in the pockets except his wallet. I took the money out of it." With a small show of defiance she added, "I've still got it, every cent. I don't want it. I'm not a thief."

"I'm sure of that, but why did you take it? I don't understand that."

She stuttered over her answer. "Why, why, I guess it was to protect myself. People wouldn't think of me as a burglar, living the way I do right here in the inn."

Again Charleston sat silent for a moment. He had lowered his gaze, and now he lifted it and looked at Rose's face, maybe to prepare her for what was to come.

What he must have seen, Perkins reflected, was a drawn and still tear-stained face and a young mouth that trembled. But go on, Charleston, he said to himself. Get it over with.

At last Charleston said, "That won't do, Rose. You're holding something back. I know that. I know that when you sat up in bed and saw the door closing, you saw who was closing it. It's best to admit it."

She was quick with her answer, too quick, Perkins thought. "I just saw a man slipping out, only the back of him. I told you I don't know who it was."

"Yes you do, Rose. Shall I say his name?"

"You weren't there. How can you know?"

Charleston took a deep breath and let it out slow. He went on, nodding to his words, not talking directly to the girl. "Young men can do crazy things when they're upset in love."

He waited until she said, "Why do you say that?"

"Yes, a young fellow in love with a girl hates the man who comes between them. He loses his head."

"I don't know anything about that."

"Oh, yes you do, Rose. We both do. We have an example before us."

She had held up bravely, Perkins thought. Tears, yes, and sobs, but still with spirit behind them. Now she drooped, the last resistance gone. Her face looked stricken, still with despair.

"It was Larry Bates, wasn't it, Rose?"

She didn't answer.

"Just tell the truth, Rose. Just say it was Larry."

"Don't beat on me. You know it, so why beat on me?" she answered in a last little flare.

"We need your confirmation, Rose. Without it we don't have a case."

"I don't care."

"And once you say it was Larry Bates, your aunt will be in the clear. Think about that."

That ruse again, that trick that went against the grain. Perkins could see dislike of it in Charleston's face.

She answered, each word slow in coming, standing by itself, "It was Larry Bates."

Charleston and Goodman waited while Inspector Perkins took Rose back to the inn.

"You're a tough interrogator," Goodman said.

"Can be, but I hate it. Acting mean makes me feel mean." Not exactly mean, he thought but somehow unworthy, as if he'd failed some test of humanity.

"Always?"

"Nope. Just with innocents like Rose."

"I guess you know you saved Inspector Perkins's hide."

"That's one satisfaction."

"And it's got my thanks with it. Perkins's, too, I know."

Constable Rendell came through the door. "Working late?" Goodman asked by way of greeting.

"Saw the lights. Thought I'd check in. What's up?"

"What's up is we're about to close the shop."

"I figured so. I heard the inspector ripping skin off of Hawley."

"It's not that. We're back in business. Case solved."

"The hell!"

"It's Larry Bates, the bus boy. We're about to put the arm on him."

"I'll be damned."

Perkins returned then. "I left her in the hands of the Witherspoon woman. She said she'd give her some hot milk and a couple of tablets. She's rather a wreck." He shrugged as if to shrug so much sympathy away. "She wanted the killing to look like a robbery. She saved every penny she took from Smith's wallet." He turned and put his hand on the doorknob. "Let's march."

As they filed out, Rendell said, "How do you want us, Inspector?"

"Not too close. Don't want to look like a delegation. Rose said it wasn't but a few minutes' walk."

The night was clear, though somewhat chilly, and the stars gave light enough for their footing. Perkins led the way. They crossed an intersection, then another, and Perkins halted in front of a small, unlighted house. He spoke in a whisper. "Rendell, sneak around and watch the back door. Goodman, stay off to one side. I'll go to the door with Charleston well behind me." He went silent for a moment, then added, "All this to-do to arrest one whelp, but you never can tell."

A patch of garden fronted the place. Charleston saw no flowers except one forlorn peony. Perkins stepped along a narrow walk to the door. He hesitated then, as if to find a bell push, gave up, and banged his fist on the door. He waited and banged again, and a light came on, and a whiny voice said through a crack in the door, "What do you want? Who is it?"

"Police. Is Larry Bates here?"

The voice answered, "Yes. No. He's sleepin'. Come back tomorrow."

"You wake him up and do it now."

"No, I won't. I just won't."

"We'll break in, then."

"Don't do that. Oh, God, he's not in trouble, is he?"

"Just wake him up."

"He's a good boy."

"Wake him up."

"He'll have to put some clothes on."

"All right. No stalling. We'll wait right here."

The night, it seemed to Charleston, had turned darker, though no clouds obscured the stars. Change in his vision, perhaps, from the light through the door to the dark outside. He heard no sounds except the little sounds of his own breathing. Somewhere a dog barked. To be in keeping, it had to be a black dog.

Then came the step-step of feet inside, and a male voice said through the door's crack, "I ain't done nothin'! Who says I did?"

"Open up."

Perkins gave a shove to the door. It swung, halted, and then swung full open. Larry Bates stood there.

"All right, Bates," Perkins said. "Come along."

"What's wrong? I said I didn't do nothin'."

"Come on."

"What for?"

"To answer some questions."

"What about? I already answered your questions."

"About murders. About Oliver Smith. About Constable Doggett."

The boy did a blind bolt, charging straight ahead. For a bare instant Charleston was put in mind of a loco horse. Bates knocked Perkins sprawling and ran toward Charleston. Charleston dodged aside and put a foot out. Bates tripped, seemed to soar, and fell flat on his face. Almost as he fell, Goodman was on him. Charleston helped with the handcuffs.

Bates quit struggling. He cried into the ground, "Oh, Jesus! Oh, you bloody buggers."

From the doorway his mother screamed, "What you doin' with my boy? Stop it. Leave him be. Stop it, I said."

Rendell returned from the back of the house. Perkins said to him, "Hush her up if you can. Tell her we won't hurt him, just ask some questions. Anything."

Bates was crying quietly. He trudged along with them to the incidents room and sat down when told to. Goodman removed the handcuffs.

Perkins took his time before saying, "You're entitled to legal help if you want it. You can make a phone call. And you can keep silent, not answering our questions, if that's your choice. And I caution you that what you say may be used against you. Understood?"

"I don't want none of that."

"All right. We have evidence that you drove a knife into Mr. Smith's back."

Bates wiped his nose with the back of his hand and raised wet eyes. There was dirt on his face from his fall. "What will happen to me?" he asked, as if an answer might come from the air.

"That's for a jury and judge to decide. We can't say."

"I'll tell 'em he deserved killin' like he did. That's what I'll say."

"Why?"

"He took away my girl, don't you see? And he was ruinin' her. He was ruinin' Rose. That's why I killed him."

"The jury may think that's not enough reason."

Bates flung up his hands and cried out, "Ain't there no right in this world? Who says I done wrong?"

Charleston put in quietly, "Why don't you tell us more about it, Larry?"

Bates had his hands in his lap now. "He was havin' Rose on. I knew that."

"It seems she was willing."

"That was how he was ruinin' her." Bates spoke with renewed heat. "Don't you see? I waited until I caught 'em together, then I pushed the knife in him, and God himself will say I done right."

Goodman looked up from his notes, shaking his head at what he had heard.

Charleston bent forward. "Then you killed Doggett? Did you find that killing easier after the first one?"

"It weren't easy, and I didn't want to do it, but there was nothin' else for it. I had to."

"Had to?"

"He was onto me."

Perkins took over. "Tell us about that."

Bates swallowed while he hunted for words. "That night. You know, that night."

"The night you killed Mr. Smith?"

"I told you he had it coming." There was some defiance there yet.

"Yes. Yes. Go on."

"That night, it was late, and Doggett saw me leaving the inn."

"He was suspicious?"

"No. Not then. He asked me what I was doin', leavin' the inn so late, and I had to make up a story. I told him I had forgot some medicine I bought for my mother from the chemist's and had to come back to get it."

"That satisfied him?"

"I guess so, until later. Then he must have started thinkin' on it, and he went to the chemist who told him different."

Perkins looked toward Charleston and said as an aside, "Score one for Doggett. That's what he wanted." Then, to Bates, "Tell us the rest."

"He asked me to meet him at his place that night, Doggett did. He didn't say what he wanted, but he sounded like he had something on me. So I sneaked around to his house, and he told me about goin' to the chemist and said that was proof I was guilty, and he kind of laughed and said he'd show you smart men something, and there was that little bat there, and I took it and swung it hard as I could."

The rush of words seemed to have been too much for Bates. He took a long, shuddering breath and put his head in his hands.

It crossed Charleston's mind that Doggett had thought to redeem himself by solving the Smith murder all on his own, the poor bungler.

Perkins said to all of them, "That seems to be it."

"One question for the record," Charleston said. "Bates, how did you get back into the inn the night you killed Smith?"

Bates said through his hands as if the point didn't matter, "I just made out to lock the back door, that's all. Simple."

Perkins came to his feet. "That's enough for tonight. Go along with Sergeant Goodman. I'm talking to you, Bates. Rendell, maybe you'd better go along with them."

Goodman put his notes aside. "If he wants to, but I can handle it."

When they had gone, Perkins said, "Chick, I want to know what tipped you off?"

"Sure thing. Young Smith gave me sort of an idea, the beginning of one. He got furious when his girlfriend said she would or could find another man. He made threats against him, whoever he might be, and I got to thinking about young love. Terrible thing, young love. All glands and no brains. Then, tonight, when I learned about Rose's affair with Oliver Smith, the two things came together, along with a third. That was Bates, moon-calfing over Rose. They would have for you if you had heard Tom Smith."

"I doubt it. And then that threat, your saying Mrs. Vaughn had to be guilty. You sure know more than one way to skin a cat."

"Now, Fred, don't call Rose a cat. Detection gone wrong, that is."

Perkins grinned, then sobered. "Going to miss you, Chick, we are. Hard for me to say how much I thank you."

"Aw, pisswillie, Fred. Skip it. Aren't you going to call headquarters?"

"Right away." Perkins lifted the phone, but before he dialed he said, "With pleasure."

Chapter Twenty-Two

ALONE IN HIS QUARTERS, Perkins sat thinking, or, as his father might have put it, thinking he was thinking. He ought to come alive, throw stuff in his bag and be ready to leave for Gloucester in the morning. Goodman would pack for him, if it came to that. That was just what he needed now he was so old, a batman.

He ought to be satisfied. Case solved. Position secure, at least for the time. Yes, satisfied but not elated. Who could rejoice, pinning a murder on a young loony. Just a bunch of muscles who thought he'd done right. All balls and no brains.

Once in a while you nailed a man who was evil all through, and then you threw your hat in the air. Not this time, though. Not this time.

So tomorrow he'd be on his way. Goodbye to Upper Beechwood. Goodbye to Chick and his wife. Soon enough they'd be only memories. Too soon. Goodbye to Drusilla if he saw her. Best maybe he didn't. Too hard to say. It wasn't a choice he was making: it was accepting the facts. It was the hardest lesson in life, maybe, this having to learn to say goodbye.

But the hell with it all. He came to his feet.

He tossed things in his suitcase, not caring about wrinkles, jammed them down to let the lid close, and fastened the latch. His briefcase was locked and all right. His watch said midnight. When you didn't know what else to do, you went to bed.

He had one shoe off when there came a soft tapping at the door. He strode to it, leaving the shoe. He looked in her face and brought her to him. "Not so sad, Dru. Please, why so sad?" She was limp and unresponsive in his arms, and she said, "I'm sorry, so sorry, Fred."

"Why?" He hadn't meant to sound demanding. "Nothing we've done?"

"Could you spare me a drink?"

"Of course," he answered, putting heartiness in his voice. "You're tired. It will boost you."

He had bought a fresh bottle, and he poured splashes into two glasses, adding ice and water to hers, and brought them in and handed one to her. "Please sit down and relax, and after a while you can tell me."

"Can't there be happy endings?" she asked, looking beyond the untouched glass in her hand.

He sat down on the bed close to her. "There can be happy times. I've had them with you."

"Yes, and that's all in the past." She went on, not looking at him, not looking at anything except space. "In the first place, it was a kind of curiosity. I think you know that, Fred. Yes, and add physical hunger to it." She hesitated, took the merest sip of her drink, and continued, still looking into space. "Then it changed for me, Fred. It was sort of magical, like a spell. I wanted to be with you. I don't mean for a sneak night or two. I wanted a lot more than that." She lifted her face to his then and asked simply, as a child might have asked, "Fred, would you have had me for keeps?"

The truth hit him, and the words poured out of themselves.

"God's sake! Would I have you? My dear, night and day, all the time, everywhere."

"Thank you, Fred." There were tears in her eyes. "Thank you, but . . ."

"What's the matter? You can get a divorce. We'll get one."

She lowered her head and shook it slowly, and a tear fell on her hand. "Oh, I wish, I wish — but it's not for us, Fred."

"Tell me why."

She nodded, put her glass on the floor and put her hand on her mouth to straighten it out. "I know he's not much of a husband, and I guess he's not honest, but doesn't a decent person answer to need?"

"I'm in the dark."

"The United States government wants him returned there to answer charges. They've filed for extradition. The lawyers called up."

"What charges?"

"I guess it's fraud. Some insurance thing. Walter is so close-mouthed. Could they — I mean we — have been traced through your murder investigation?"

There was nothing for it but an honest answer, though he was slow in giving it. "That's a possibility. I'm not sure. My headquarters was supposed to ask Washington about them. You'll have to know. I was the one who suggested Washington."

"I'm wanted, too, and the Posts." She let out a little cry. "Oh, Fred, it's such a miserable thing."

He longed to take her in his arms, to pat her shoulder as if she were a child, but something told him not to. He said, "I'm sorry for your sake."

"Don't be. You mustn't be that way. You just did what you had to do."

"I'm still sorry. You're perfectly innocent."

"That doesn't matter so much right now. Walter laughs and talks because that's his way, but underneath he's afraid, and Ben Post is cursing him for not going to South America sooner."

"Has your husband asked you to stay with him?"

"Not in words, but I can tell. He wants me close to him for a change. He keeps saying, 'We'll see this thing through, you and I, Drusilla.' He needs me, Fred. For the first time in his life he needs me, and for the first time in my life I am needed. I can't turn my back, not and feel right with myself."

"I need you, too."

"And you know I need you, but Fred, I can't make it seem right. Would you respect me?" Tears were running down her cheeks, unheeded.

"I would, regardless," he said, "but that's hardly the point. Oh, Christ, Dru. I know. You have to live with yourself. I hate it."

He got up and found a handkerchief and gave it to her. While she wiped her cheeks and eyes, she said, "Yes, even tonight. You could make love to me, Fred, but I couldn't answer to it."

A fierce impulse seized him, to take her, to plunge deep in her, to have her mouth and feel her breasts against him. He hadn't touched his drink, and he took it now in one gulp. He said, "It's all right, Dru. It's all right."

She rose quietly and moved toward the door.

"I'm not saying goodbye to hope," he told her. "I'm not saying goodbye forever."

"Thank you, Fred. Thank you, my dear."

Her shoulder trembled under his hand. She bowed her head and went out the door.

He went back and sat on the bed and looked at the closed door and let the other shoe drop.

Chapter Twenty-Three

GEETA WAS BUSY PACKING when Charleston came into the room about midnight. She put down a garment and came and kissed him, saying, "You must have had quite a day. Sit down and have some wine." A frown came on her face. "Goodness, you look tired, Chick."

"Tired but triumphant, if that's the word."

He told her then about the day, about the quizzing of Rose and the arrest of Bates, ending by saying, "It was you who found the way for me, you and your young Smith. Take some credit. Take all of it."

"I knew you'd bring it off," she said, "that is if you had time. You always do. Here's your drink and my salute."

"Yeah, and if I'd been keener, I might have saved Doggett's life."

"I don't see how."

"Me either, come to that."

"You don't seem very happy, Chick. I should think you would be."

"Just put it I'm at ease. Geeta, you ever wonder if there's any force more terrible than young love?"

She went back to her packing. "It's only natural."

"That's the hell of it. The juices begin to flow, and the kids aren't prepared for it. Not old enough. No experience. We call it puppy love when we get older and try to laugh it off, but when it happens to kids it's the realest thing in the world. It's the only thing." He laughed shortly and said, "But here I go being preacher again."

"Preach away, Reverend."

"Thanks. Until it runs its course, reason can't faze it. Advice falls flat. Sometimes it goes haywire, as in Bates's case. Sometimes it leaves scars. It always leaves memories. They can haunt you." He shook his head. "It's a lovely lunacy."

"I doubt you're going to change it, even you, and not tonight."

"Oh ye of little faith."

She was folding things just so, patting out wrinkles, finding the right places for them, and humming as she worked.

"Put words to it," he asked.

"To what?"

"To that tune."

"I've been thinking that pretty soon now we'll have our own mountains and our own glens and braes, and I've been changing some words in a Scottish song."

"Well, sing it."

"I can't and go on packing."

"Oh, sing it, Geeta."

Her voice came out low and clear:

> "For these are my mountains,
> And this is my glen.
> The scenes of my childhood
> Will know me again.
> No land's ever claimed me
> Though far I did roam,
> For these are my mountains,
> And I'm going home."

"Thanks, dear. Yep, home. Montana."

"But London first," she said. "I do hope the hotel will take us. I suppose it's too late for a reservation."

"No need," he told her. "I called the Chesterfield. It's okay."

"I might have known, Chick. Aren't you getting excited? London and then home, and I'll think of the gray stone of Edinburgh and the woolens there, and this lovely Cotswold country, and I'll get impish and say 'Fie on Ben Nevis. Look to our Rockies.' "

He came to his feet and said, "You've done enough."

"I'm just through."

"Time for bed, and you know what?"

"Stop it. I know what, all right. And you, you lecher, speaking of puppy love!"

"I'm a kid again."

"It's too late."

"Never too late. Please."

She gave him her good smile and began undressing.

Chapter Twenty-Four

As THEY FINISHED BREAKFAST the next morning, Charleston said, "I want to dodge over and tell Perkins goodbye. I'll check out first, and then will you see if you can round up the bellman and get the things in the car? May be difficult with all the tourists."

"I can manage, but I want to say goodbye to Mr. Ebersole. He's sent the flow-blue on and wouldn't take even a dime for expenses."

"Hold that for the last. I want to thank him myself."

All hands were present when he opened the door to the incidents room, all hands including Superintendent Hawley. He barely had time to close it before Hawley barked, "My congratulations, Mr. Charleston. Fine work."

"Me? Congratulations? No, sir. They belong to Inspector Perkins and to Goodman and Rendell."

"But Perkins was by way of saying you broke the case."

Charleston laughed. "Isn't that just like him? Generous with credits to everyone but himself. No, Superintendent, don't you believe him. If he hadn't insisted on questioning Rose Whaley again and again, we'd never have gotten to the bottom of this business. To tell the truth, I thought he was a bit daft, as you British might put it.

"You can be sure, sir," he went on against Hawley's sputter, "that I had little to do with the solution. In fact, they've given me quite an education, this fine team of yours. I'm going to write to your Chief Constable telling him about Perkins and the work of Goodman and Rendell. I think he might like an American's impressions. And don't you think it would be a good idea to sent a copy to Scotland Yard? I want to show my appreciation."

Sergeant Goodman, all innocence, suggested brightly, "The Home Office?"

"Oh, yes. The Home Office. And the newspapers, if reporters come around."

He didn't wait for an answer, but reached out and pumped the limp hand. "I have to be going. My wife's waiting." He shook hands then with Goodman and Rendell and, last of all, with Perkins. Perkins moved closer to him as their hands met. With his left hand he grasped Charleston's shoulder. "Chick, you, you . . ." The handclasp was strong, but the voice unsteady. "Well, goddamnit, goodbye."

Halfway across the street Charleston turned. They had all come out and were standing in front of the door, all but Hawley. He waved to them once and swung about and went on toward the car, where the bellman was stowing the last of the luggage and Geeta stood waiting.

It was a nice morning in the Cotswolds.